GREAT BRITISH HORROR III

FOR THOSE IN PERIL

Great British Horror III
For Those in Peril

Edited by
Steve J Shaw

BLACK
SHUCK
BOOKS

First published in Great Britain in 2018 by

Black Shuck Books
Kent, UK

978-1-913038-05-2

This one's for my dad – hey old man, sorry it's a bit late

The Seas of the Moon
Georgina Bruce

The first card she turned. The drowned sailor.

Those are pearls that were his eyes.

Buried treasure. Secrets to be divined.

That moment when the tide ran back, revealing the bodies caught out in the treacherous cove. Drowned mouths all open and full of sand.

The soft slide and tang of an oyster as she swallowed. Tasting the sea. Seasick, sliding around in her guts. She wrapped the cards in a square of soft green silk and put them away in her pocket. Looked out over the calm water, beyond the rocky shore. The slosh of sea in the bowl of her stomach.

Under the ocean, all of the drowned. All of the dead souls glittered with nacre, growing a hard pearly sheen.

A ferry from one shore to another. No choice. Everything broken now, like a crack across the top of her head.

They'd never forgive her.

Getting into trouble. Getting out of it again. They'd never forgive her either way.

The rain started up, hard and heavy, a rain of stones and gravel, bullets and nails. She ran to the covered seating area and listened to the rain bouncing off the deck of the ferry. Couldn't see much through the grey blur, the wet broken lights moving about her in psychedelic blobs of colour. The shadowy sea storming under black clouds.

She'd slipped out in the middle of the night, taking nothing but her passport, her cards, a packet of her dad's cigarettes, and her granny's pearls. They're worth something, her gran had whispered. Knowing that she wouldn't go back, she felt she had no right to take anything else. She left her phone, so they couldn't track her that way. Maybe they wouldn't notice she was gone, for a while at least. Maybe even long enough to lose herself on the other side on the ocean. Would they really bother coming after her, all this way? After this, there was no going back, even if she wanted to. No going back to her Dad with his belt, and the priest with his fat mouth, or her Mam with her hard unforgiving silence, and her brothers with their mocking cries of *witch*, *witch*, *bitch*. No going back to Conor. Slight and serious, innocent Conor. He would say she'd broken his heart. He'd cry and call her cruel, evil and unnatural. She was, she was all those things, and she was so, so sorry... but then. If she went back. Then, all possible futures would collapse into one predictable dull layer of drudgery and routine. Teeth at her breasts. Sticky fingers in her hair. No, no she didn't want any of that. Pathetic as it might be, small and pointless as everyone said it was. Still. Whatever. She wanted her life for herself.

For all its ugly bulk, the ferry seemed high and fragile, hanging over tumultuous waters. The sea snapping from below, foaming mouth and hands and teeth – Siobhan couldn't shake the idea that she was to be punished. One way or another. How much did she even believe in that place, anyway? A place of no judgement, where she'd be cut free from that tiny clump of cells growing to a heavy iron ball and chain. Could it really be so simple? But don't think about that. Think too much and you won't have the courage.

The rain and sea spray smashed against the side of the boat; water sluiced over the deck. She felt sick again, and ran to the railings to lean over and spit bile into the ocean. Her granny's pearls hanging from her neck. The wind lashed and caught them, and they split from their fragile thread and fell, one by one, away into the sea.

She watched for lightning and counted the seconds until the thunder. Miles away! Inside the house was cold, the fire small and the floors bare. The boys were out in the storm, drawn to the smash and drama of the cliffs. Siobhan was inside, dandling a sleepy baby on her hip. The child was exhausted from crying but it wouldn't sleep; it woke itself up every few seconds to mewl and pet.

Quiet yourself down, snapped Siobhan. Her mind was elsewhere, watching the garden through the window. The garden was sodden, mud-ridden, a drenched green blur. Something pale moved under the bushes, something soft like a little white baby. Siobhan pressed her forehead to the glass and tried to focus. Something small and whitish was curled under the woody rhododendron bush. But when she blinked she lost focus and couldn't see it anymore; maybe it was rubbish, washed away by the rain.

A new wave of thunder broke over the sky, and lightning followed a few moments later. Close by, now. It rained harder, rain bounced off the window, bored holes into the mud of the garden, drummed up worms. Another roll of thunder came barrelling in, this one shaking the sky, cracking open the earth, and bringing its own nuclear flash of light. The trees blared green for a second, the black sky making a negative of itself. The baby screamed and Siobhan jiggled it up and down on her hip. For a second she thought she saw its bones through the pale illuminated flesh. Little skeleton.

Where were the boys? Oh, gone down to the beach. Don't tell Conor she'd let them go out in this weather. They'd come back cold, with sand in their hair and lashes, and skin chapped by the storm, their hands full of pebbles and clams and crabs. Bloodied knees. Walking mud all over her clean floors.

Distant tower blocks looked like ships bobbing up and down on the slate-grey churning sea. Siobhan smoked two cigarettes, lighting the second from the end of the first. Stubbed them out under her foot and went back to her bed on the ward.

The doctor had been to see her earlier that day. *Grand news, we were able to save the baby.* His smile like a thin pecking beak. He'd patted her hand. *Come along, there's nothing to worry about.*

The ward was quiet now. Siobhan spread her cards

across the bed and picked one at random. The Emperor. Seated on his throne, with his staff and his orb. The whole world was his. She always turned that card lately, feeling guilty for the rules she'd broken, the order she'd defied. It was Dad, in his Sunday best, quoting from the bible. He whipped her with his belt but took no pleasure in it. He did what must be done, upright and rigid and placid as stone. She'd say this card was God Himself, the holy patriarch. Except no, God was wild and furious. The terror. He was out to get her, to drag his claws over her and haul her back into his cave.

He'd come for her on the boat. He was a shape at first, a slow emergence, pushing under the water. And then he was a bear, a huge bear, ten times bigger than the boat. Bigger than the sky. His fur snagged with green strands and globules of seaweed. His teeth dripped saltwater from jagged yellow points. He took the boat in his two great paws and lifted it high. Siobhan clinging to the railings, screaming, scrabbling as her feet slid away from under her. Couldn't hold on any longer. She felt herself falling, the boat smashed to pieces around her, and then she was submerged in shocking cold, fighting back the sea that touched with teeth and stinging flesh, and clinging weeds and scraping metal ruins. Deep breath of sea in her lungs, and she sank down, down, under the weight of water. Bear tasted her on the sea's tongue and hooked her with his claw. And her blood ballooned around her, a shining bell of crimson, a teardrop, raining to red mist. And with it a sound, a slow deep boom, the thrumming pulse of her body bursting. Bloodshimmer in the water, bloodshimmer and bloodshine.

Deep under the sea, deep and deeper, the sea that buzzed and crushed her like a muscle, the sea all haunted with roars and gulls. Under the sea, the moon wobbled like a fat white lump of flesh. And the bear devoured the boat and its passengers. He swam in circles, blood bubbling from his enormous nostrils, lashing out with his powerful limbs. Snagging the moon on his claw. The last thing Siobhan remembered before waking in the hospital: the moon hanging on the bear's claw, his sharp-toothed smile shining with pearls.

When the rain eased up, Siobhan put the baby down and went into the back garden. She searched under the rhododendron bush for the small soft white thing she'd seen. There was nothing there, nothing but leaf litter and mud, little black beetles, thin transparent worms, fat flies.

It was foolish to look, foolish to hope. Something she'd sworn she'd given up. After all the treatments, the medications, the bible study and the prayer – why look now for something more? Because the cards told her to look? But that was no reason. She'd promised Conor that she'd burned the cards, she'd sworn up and down and on the lives of her children. She'd knelt with him and prayed for forgiveness. But it had been a lie, one of many. All an illusion.

The cards – yes, she should have burned them like she'd sworn she would. The cards were evil, Conor was right. They'd taught her to look for another life, a life she'd lost at sea, or so she dreamed. She knew it was wrong, it was foolish. But she couldn't stop herself from looking.

It was the Moon she loved. Over and over it was the Moon. Ever since the time in the hospital, ever since they held her down and those babies had come tearing out of her. It was the Moon, calling and beguiling.

She'd seen it in the garden in the rain. The Moon, its madness, resting under the rhododendron bush like a big white grub. The Moon dragging a tide of blood back and forth through her body. The Moon with all its seas; she knew them off by heart and recited them in her mind: *the Sea of Bears, the Sea of Hands, the Sea of Witches, the Sea of Ghosts, the Sea of Smoke, the Sea of Blood, the Sea of Lies, the Sea of Tears, the Sea of Absence, the Sea of Murders, the Sea of Pearls, the Sea of Forgetting...*

But there was no moon under the rhododendron bush. There was nothing in the garden but mud and green. It began to rain again, and the baby's wailing started up from inside the house. After a while the sound became almost soothing, a repetitive loop, like the cry of a bird swooping high over the waves.

How could you, how could you? The devil must've been in you.

Aye, the devil alright. Squirming and gestating. Pushing out her flesh in a distorted lump, feeding from her blood. Parasitic, hungry little devil.

Towards the end she was exhausted. She knew of course the child would be a boy, another male to square off at the prison door. They would all be boys, all her children. And when it came, the pain of labour was unimaginable. Annihilating. Worse than the bear's mouth. Worse than anything. This was a tearing open of her centre, her intimate self split and turned inside out. Blood, an ocean of it. So much they had to pump her full of it again, over and over. But the child was strong. Robust and demanding.

The lungs of him! Her mother said, cradling him to her bosom.

Keep him, Siobhan said. I don't want him. But no one heard her over the sound of her baby's screams. Only the moon, peering in through the window. Only the moon seemed strange, seemed hopeful. But perhaps that was an illusion too. They gave her medicine, a lot of different medicine, and at times it drove the illusion away. But always it came back, the insistent sly thought that this wasn't real at all. That this was a dream. And her real life – that was elsewhere, happening without her.

How long had she been standing out there in the rain? She'd lost track of herself for a time. Now all at once she was aware of the silence beneath the downpour. The baby – it had stopped crying. Siobhan was drenched, her clothes heavy with rainwater, rain dragging at her skin. Her hair like rivulets of blood running from her scalp. How long had she been standing there? She couldn't tell. Where were the boys? Down at the beach, playing their daredevil games on the rocks. She'd go and call them back, get them inside before Conor came home.

She ran her hands through her soaked hair, squeezed out rivers of water. Went quickly out the back gate and down the narrow hedged-in path to the beach. I've left the baby crying, Siobhan thought. Have I? But the thought was distant, a whisper in the back of her mind. She stumbled down to the rocky cove where the boys always played. Something different there. Something not right. The boys weren't there, she couldn't even hear their voices.

Something dead on the beach.

Dead things washed up in the cove all the time. Driftwood and dead things. Shells with intricate inner staircases. Bits of broken shell and sea glass and bloated drowned things brought by the tide.

But the bear's head was bigger than all that.

Big as a church. Bigger. His neck torn away and trailing broken spine and gobbets of flesh and pouring blood into the ocean. Eyes like two black voids in the wet fur of his face. Jaws wide, a mouth ribbed like a cathedral, teeth yellow and dripping with seaweed. It was a mountain of fur and flesh and bone. Dead. Washed up. Here of all places.

Down, down the rocks, over the sand and shingle, she scraped and staggered. Down towards the great wide jaws of the bear's head. Feeling tiny, minuscule, dwarfed by his giant eyes. Bigger even than she remembered, bigger than in her dreams. The teeth she remembered well, would never forget. Razor sharp and merciless. But he was pitiful now, wasn't he? His head ripped away from his body. His powers all gone.

She saw herself approaching, reflected in his black unseeing eyes. She looked vague and ghostlike as a dream. Watched herself crouch low, hands trailing the sand and blood and surf at her feet. Felt with her fingers, dug and felt around until she found those soft little faces with their eyes and mouths and noses full of wet sand. Their small bodies crushed under the bear's weight.

And there. Nubs of ivory nestled in the weeds between its horrible teeth. Those are pearls that were her eyes. Her eyes, her bones, her heart, her life.

The sea smashed into the side of the ferry. Its voice hard with fury. Snatching at the sky.

It was only sheer luck that she caught the pearls falling from her neck, caught them in her hands and gathered them to her throat. She pulled back from the railings, let the pearls fall into her palms.

Behind her, under the shelter, children played. Climbing over the seats, hitting each other on the arms and legs. A strange feeling passed over her then. Something lost and broken. The sound of small boys playing, voices caught on the wind; it stirred something in her, some unfathomable feeling. But it passed. She stuffed the broken string of pearls into her pocket. Soon, soon, the land came into view.

Stepping Out

Kit Power

Emma was out on the deck, shivering from the cold air whipping around her, when she saw the man climb over the railing and drop into the sea.

She was maybe twenty or thirty feet away when it happened. She'd been walking the decks for ten minutes, hoping the cold would settle her stomach. The char-grilled steak had been delicious, but she'd found herself unable to adjust to the gentle movement of the boat (*ship*, Mark insisted in her mind, annoyed, *this is too big to be a boat, it's a ship*), and when the cheesecake dessert had arrived, the sight of it had turned her stomach and she'd had to excuse herself. Mumbling that she felt seasick, she'd pulled her hand from Mark's with an effort, and rushed out of the restaurant.

She'd started shivering almost at once, her dress and thin cardigan providing little protection from the cutting northerly breeze. She welcomed the cold driving away the nausea, her stomach and throat clenching against the idea of losing precious body heat. The deck was virtually empty, and she resolved to make at least one complete circuit to clear her head and make sure her tummy had settled properly.

She'd made it down one side of the ship, across the aft

(stopping briefly to admire the churn in the ocean as the huge motor pushed them across the cold darkness) and back up the far side. Her pace had begun to slow, as she realised she was getting nearer to where she'd started and would have to return. She could feel a low-level anxiety building as she imagined having to deal with Mark's parents' over-solicitous concerns, and his resentment at being left. She'd begun the wary mental task of rehearsing what she might say to try and placate him when she saw the door open ahead, and the man walk through.

He was wearing a black tuxedo (even though formal night wasn't until Wednesday, and boy, was she looking forward to *that* particular shit show, with its limitless opportunity for crippling *faux pas*) and had a handsome, tanned face topped with close-cut dark hair. He moved slowly and easily over to the railing, hands in his pockets. Emma's eyes followed him, enjoying the confidence of his stride. He looked like he *belonged* in this strange floating town centre/shopping mall/posh-eatery miniature world – like he might actually live here, spending every morning in the pool or gym, taking cocktails in the afternoon, fine dining in the evening. People did, she imagined – retirees with unimaginable pensions, choosing to see things out in style, in comfort, and on the move.

But he was too young for that, she reckoned, and too carefree. Some trust fund child, then, perhaps aristocracy, even? As she contemplated his background, he reached the railing, and without breaking stride, swung one leg over.

Emma froze in place, her breath catching in her throat. She was aware of her pulse pounding all at once, thudding in her ears. Her mind was frozen too, stuck in the calmness with which the scene was unfolding. Nothing in his body language had indicated stress, confusion, or intoxication. He'd swung the leg over as calmly and naturally as a cyclist might board a bike. He sat now on the railing, the central bar between his legs, and looked directly at her. His eyes were dark brown, and seemed calm, even friendly.

He smiled at her, winked, then, just as casually, he swung the other leg over the bar, let go of the railing, and plunged immediately out of view.

Emma felt as though the deck had lurched under her feet. She staggered over to the wall and leant against it, panting. The metal was ferociously cold against her skin, and the pain served to keep her away from the edge she felt she was suddenly teetering on. She couldn't stop staring at the spot on the railing where the man had sat. She felt, in some stupid way, that if she kept staring, he would come back. Or that she'd suddenly see him just sitting there, her mind having somehow imagined him falling.

The railing remained stubbornly empty. She rubbed her eyes, feeling the chill of her fingers against her closed eyelids, but when she looked again, the railing was still bare. As though he'd never been there.

Had he been there?

It seemed a ridiculous question, but the longer she stared at the railing, the more the unreality of the entire event began to sink in. She replayed it in her mind – his suit, his easy stroll, the wink, the smile, the drop...

There was no splash!

The thought bubbled up in her mind, and she held it. As she did, her mind replayed the whole incident.

She felt her head spinning, and a shudder ran through her. She had to get off this deck, now.

She was sat at the bar, nursing her second large brandy, staring into space. She'd spoken only to order the drinks, otherwise concentrating on getting warm and not thinking. She'd take a sip, feel the drink warm her. Try to focus on the buttery taste, to just breathe. Then she'd see the man, winking and smiling, and she'd feel blankness crowding in, threatening to sweep her away. She'd take another sip. Breathe.

"Emma?" By the time the second brandy was halfway down, she was feeling calmer, and was managing longer and longer stretches of full consciousness, so it took her a couple of seconds to recognize her own name, and another couple more before she was able to place Mark's voice. His tone was that faux-relaxed one he used when he was angry in public – soft, cloying. It made her stomach cramp, the brandy suddenly burning rather than warming, in her gut and on her lips.

"Mark, hi…" She trailed off, uncertain how to continue. The image of the man in the tux bubbled up, and she felt a dizziness in her head, like a plughole had opened there, draining her away. She couldn't begin to find the words.

"Having a good time, are you? That's nice, love." He took a seat next to her, flicking his hand at the bartender, dismissing his approach. "Feeling better?" He was smiling his angry grin, and the dizziness amplified. Her lips and tongue felt thick, almost numb.

"Yeah, no, I... sorry, I just... I didn't mean to slope off, I was just..."

"You weren't feeling well, were you? That's okay, I'm sure mum and dad will understand. They've spent all this money, of course they'd want you to have a good time." So soft, his voice pitched low, his body language relaxed, but God he was furious. The dig about the money reminded her of the endless conversations before the trip about being grateful, not embarrassing them both, and she flashed back with vivid clarity to the blazing row in the car on the way to Dover, which had led to 60 miles of sullen silence; him driving too fast, her looking out of the window, trying not to cry.

"I'm not..." She saw the way he tilted his head, and changed course "...I mean, I *am* having a good time, of course, I just..."

"Good! Then all's right with the world! Brandy settled your stomach?" He'd already slipped off the barstool and stood next to her, a step behind. Telling her it was time to leave.

"No, yeah, I don't feel sick any more..."

"Good! That's good. Well, come on, drink up. Then we can get an early night, make a proper start on things in the morning." He was still smiling, but she could see the effort it was taking, and the sullen fury behind it. She swallowed nervously, looking back to the brandy. She'd ordered doubles, and there was still a generous amount left in the glass. She looked back up at him, and he just nodded, making a *hurry up* gesture with his hand.

She lifted the glass to her lips, took a deep breath, and swallowed the drink down in three gulps. It burned her throat, and she felt pain in her stomach. Her eyes were watering as she tried not to choke, and the glass rattled on the bar as she put it down. Mark took her hand, gripping tight enough to hurt, and pulled her off the barstool.

She went away again, briefly, on the short walk back to the cabin. When she returned to herself, her hand was crushed in his grip, fingers painfully mashed together. He finally released her to open their door, putting his arm around her as if to guide her in, then pushing her in the small of the back once she was inside the room. She staggered forwards a few steps, overbalanced on her high heels, and fell face forward onto the bed. As she rolled over and sat up, she heard the door shut, and Mark's voice asking "Fucking hell, how many have you had?"

She looked up at him, saw the anger blazing in his eyes, his scowl, and looked quickly back down at her feet. "Just a couple of brandies, that's all..."

"Charged them to the room, of course. You know we're paying for that, right? Mum and Dad aren't made of money. I know they're treating us to the holiday but..."

"I know, you said..." She picked at the ankle strap of her shoe, trying to unthread the annoyingly thin strap from the buckle.

"Well, then take it fucking easy, would you?" He spoke over her, his voice still low and conversational, but fizzing with disgust. "Jesus, they'd sprung for the bottle of wine, that wasn't good enough for you? You had to slink off and hit the spirits?"

"It wasn't like that—"

"Fucking looked a lot like it to me. I know you don't really like them—"

"I do, I—"

"—oh, don't give me that shit, you can't stand them, never have—"

"—that's not fair, I—"

"Fair? You want to talk about fairness? What's fair about you pissing off in the middle of dessert to get hammered at the bar, because that's how much you can't stand being around them?" He was close now, kneeling in front of her, hands on her knees, under her skirt. She looked into his eyes. And she felt what had happened welling up inside her... but the knot of his brow, the tightness of his jaw, silenced her.

She *didn't* like them, that was the thing. She didn't like the way they were with each other, constantly sniping, vicious comments disguised as humor. She didn't like how they drank too much, every single social occasion, how they seemingly couldn't socialize at all without booze. She struggled with their ostentatious generosity, how it felt to her that they always squeezed every last drop of thanks out of her for every gift or favour bestowed, and how she would be left each time with the uneasy sense that they felt she was somehow ungrateful.

She *didn't* like them, and Mark knew her well enough to tell, no matter how hard she tried to hide it. It fed a near constant resentment, always bubbling under the surface. It made her sad and wore her down. Her mind pulled back towards the man in the suit. Had she really seen it? Had she not? And if she had, why hadn't she said anything? Why didn't she...

"We've got eight days. Please don't ruin it by being a bitch, okay?"

The word stung her, brought her back to herself with a thud. His voice had further softened, like he was trying to make up, his reasonable-adult voice. She felt herself blushing.

"I'm sorry." The words were dull, and she felt a wave of listlessness roll over her as she was saying them. He smiled up at her then. "Thank you. Let's just try and make the most of it, yeah?" As he said this, his hands slid up her thighs, to her hips, and his mouth to her cleavage.

Five minutes later, he was inside her, thrusting. Ten minutes later, he was snoring. She lay on her back, feeling what he'd left behind trickle down her thigh and onto her dress, and the soreness in her breasts where he'd squeezed.

His snores kept her awake a long time, and her broken sleep was filled with dreams of smiling, winking, handsome strangers in tuxedos, and the dark, pounding, endless ocean.

The man followed her for the rest of the holiday. She saw him whenever she closed her eyes, whenever her focus wandered, which was more and more as the trip progressed. Sleep remained elusive and fragmentary, and between that and the free-flowing booze (mostly bought by Mark's parents, of course, with great fanfare), she found herself more and more in a fugue state – numb and indifferent.

Mark's ardour seemed undaunted by her apathy – in fact, she began to suspect he was in some way encouraged by it, taking her lack of interest in arguing about it (as she sometimes would at home, when pushed), as incitement, an opportunity... Or maybe he'd convinced himself this really was a romantic holiday, and the environment had somehow increased her libido. She submitted to his advances with neither enthusiasm nor resistance, even as he became increasingly adventurous, initiating positions they'd never done before – or even talked about. He'd even fucked her in the disabled toilet next to the bar, on the evening of the fifth day. That had been frantic but over quickly, his excitement overwhelming him just as her body had begun to loosen up, to accommodate him properly. It made her sore, but she didn't really mind.

Nothing really seemed to matter.

Mark didn't matter, his parents didn't matter, his petty dirty advances didn't matter. She'd listened out, again and again, for some kind of announcement, some notification that someone had gone missing, had gone overboard, but there was nothing.

That mattered. Or did it? It must happen all the time, she realised – or, at least, fairly often. People just... going missing. Often enough that you wouldn't want to ruin everyone else's holiday with it. Or had it *not* really happened? But it had been so vivid. *He* had been so vivid.

She thought about him all the time. The easy roll of his shoulders as he walked, the glimpse of white teeth as he smiled. The memory refused to fade, remaining stubbornly clear and distinct, no matter how many times she thought about it, as she tried to sleep, or tried to laugh with Mark's parents, or tried to take her mind off Mark climbing on top of her, into her. The memory took her miles away from whatever was going on around her. Into a blessed blankness where nothing mattered.

On the final day of the cruise, they stood together at one of the poolside bars. Emma sat safely behind her shades as Mark's parents bemoaned the return to normality, and insisted on ordering one more round – 'No, no, love, our treat, really' – in order to 'make the most' of the few hours left on board.

"Have you had a good time, dear?"

Mark's mother was facing her, sunglasses concealing her eyes, seeming to stare at her instead with her puckered lips, the light pink smear of lipstick against her tanned and leathery skin seeming obscene to Emma – like seeing the intimate areas of a lizard.

"It's been wonderful, I can't thank you enough," she said, speaking straight to those trembling lips.

"Ah, you're welcome dear, we've loved being able to do it, just this once. It's what it's all about, isn't it? Family. Right, Ted?"

"More like all about getting hammered and eating like a pig," Mark's dad chuckled. Mark, mid-sip, spat a mouthful of lager back into his glass and belly-laughed. Emma didn't look, staying focused on his mother. The lips pursed even tighter, almost disappearing, her mouth now looking for all the world like a cat's anus, Emma thought, managing not to smile.

"Ignore him, dear, he doesn't appreciate the finer things."

"Oh, I appreciate 'em, but it's been a while..."

Mark laughed louder, and his mother swatted at his arm.

"Don't you encourage him!" She gave an exasperated shake of her head and turned back to Emma. "See what you've got to look forward to?"

Emma couldn't entirely suppress the shudder.

"Anyway. Glad you've enjoyed it, love. I know it'll be sad to get home, but remember..."

At that moment, the tannoy announced that they were entering British waters and an impromptu, embarrassing cheer went up from the crowd at the bar, including Mark and his parents... and all of a sudden, like a wave hitting her, Emma finally understood – or thought she did. She turned to Mark and gripped his hand, smiling.

"I'm going to go walk the deck, okay?"

He frowned, and glanced back at the bar, his parents. "You don't...I mean, do you want me to...?"

"No, you stay here, look after my drink. Won't be long. I just want to say goodbye to the... the ship."

"Okay."

He turned away, shoulders relaxing.

She walked away from the poolside bar heading for the front (*Bow? Stern? Bow, surely?*) of the boat, feeling the sunlight on her skin like a kiss. A kiss from a handsome stranger in a tux, perhaps. She smiled to herself. After a few minutes, she reached the nose of the ship, and stood with the crowd who were taking in the white cliffs – chattering, laughing, snapping photos. She took one herself, on an iPad, for an elderly British couple. They thanked her in strong London accents.

On the far side of the boat, the deck was empty. No-one was interested in looking out to sea.

Emma was. She stared out across the expanse – white-tipped spikes of rolling water, all the way to the edge of the sky. The cool breeze caressed her, rippling her clothes against her body.

And she saw him again – in her mind's eye. He sauntered up to the railing she leant against. She imagined a whiff of sweet aftershave. This time, when he swung his leg over the railing, she did the same. She sat on the railing, face-to-face with her memory of him. He smiled. She smiled back. He winked. She winked back.

From behind her, as if from a TV in the next room, she heard shouts, raised voices. They didn't matter.

None of it mattered.

They fell from the railing together.

The Bells of Rainey

Simon Bestwick

The boat rode up and down in the brown-grey swell. Monica felt queasy; the summer heat-haze turned the receding coast into a dim smudged blur, so there was only the sea to look at, and its colour, together with the oily film on the surface, put her in mind of doner meat, greasy and cheap.

Dead fish bumped against the hull. The boat advertised itself as the Rainey Island Ferry, but was basically a fishing boat and smelt like one; that, and the way it rocked in the waves only increased Monica's nausea, and made the sea seem bigger and more threatening.

Stuart's hand covered hers on the rail. "You okay, love?"

She nodded. At least the shoals of dead fish were thinning – just out of Morecambe the water had turned a startling crimson, filled with dead sea-creatures of every kind; a red tide, Stuart had called it. It made Monica recall a passage from Revelations, and she moved closer to Stuart's comforting warmth. "Good job we don't believe in omens."

"Hm?"

"Omens. You know, seas turning to blood and all that?"

"Yeah." He laughed. "Lucky we don't."

Monica drew closer to him and said nothing. The ferryman glanced at Stuart, but stayed silent too.

The island rose out of the water ahead, a low hump of green and brown. The buildings in the village, painted white and pink, varied the colour a little, and Monica saw the dull grey stump of the castle at the south end.

The island grew larger, more distinct as the ferryman accelerated; soon they were entering the shallow bay, and pulling in alongside a wooden jetty jutting out from the mud and pebble beach.

The Islands of Furness dot the waters of England's north-west coast. Ramsey and Barrow Island have long been absorbed into the town of Barrow's docks system; of the others, Walney is the largest, with another nine islands and islets scattered around it.

Three miles southwest of Walney, at the mouth of Morecambe Bay and the edge of the Irish Sea, lies the remotest of the islands: a crescent-shaped accretion of silt and glacial till, two miles long and, at its thickest, three-quarters of a mile wide, called Rainey.

There are a handful of cottages and two small churches. A pub called the Commodore's Rest is the only establishment on the island offering either overnight accommodation or a place to dine. That, along with the tall peak of Dog Fell and the ruined fortress to the south, completes the list of Rainey's few attractions.

Monica's walking shoes stuck to the threadbare carpet of the Commodore's Rest, and an odour of stale cigarettes clung to the walls and furniture. The overpriced soft drinks were tepid and flat; her glass had a greasy thumbprint on it and Stuart's a smudgy trace of lipstick around the brim. Despite the hot summer's day, they left the drinks untouched and departed, having struck 'pub lunch' off their list of planned activities. Instead, they bought bottled water from the Tanker's Off-Licence and climbed Dog Fell.

The view from the peak was another disappointment: to the east, the village's rooftops blocked out what view there was, while the westward prospect overlooked the island's sewage outfall. A pipe jutted a hundred or so yards out to sea; a dull orange stain spread around it, and washed back to shore with the tide. Monica could smell it even from there.

Dog Fell wasn't a particularly challenging climb; by the time they came back down, little more than half an hour had passed since they'd landed on Rainey. The ferry left every three hours, leaving them with two and a half to kill, and a ramble around the island's coast as the only remaining activity on offer.

Rainey, as a whole, turned out to be a classic example of being better to travel hopefully than to arrive. They made their way southward to Rainey Castle; little remained of it except the outer walls, which were too precarious to climb. They walked once around the outside, again around the interior, and that was that.

Next they made their way along the western shore, avoiding the beach and breathing through their mouths due to the sewage outlet's proximity; they rounded Rainey's northernmost point with better than an hour and a half still to go. As they began the trek south, Stuart pointed out a scattered group of people on a small headland nearby, just visible beyond a series of dunes. A trio of portable toilets and a number of what looked like tents had been erected: the group's members knelt in the sand and a tall thin woman with tied-back blondish hair strode back and forth, talking and gesticulating.

"Hell's that?" said Stuart. "Prayer meeting or something?"

"Don't think so," said Monica. One of the kneeling figures held a trowel.

The two of them went towards the headland. They'd been married long enough to know one another's minds – in most respects, at least. Seeing them, the tall woman turned to face them, hands on hips.

"Hi," said Stuart. The woman raised her eyebrows, clearly unimpressed; he blinked. "We saw you working," Monica said quickly; closer to, she could see that parts of what she'd taken to be dunes were in fact stone. "We were curious."

"Hm." The woman folded her arms and looked Monica up and down; Monica could almost feel Stuart's annoyance at the snub. Then the other woman turned and barked at one of her workers. "Jesus Christ, Stefan, shore the goddamned sand up before you get buried alive."

Stefan, a boy of about nineteen, blinked at the dune in front of him, nodded and grabbed a wooden board. The workers, all in their teens or twenties, were digging their way into the dunes, erecting wooden boards to stop the sand falling back in, and were clearing the sand from what looked like stubs of masonry.

"Always good to meet an enquiring mind," the woman said; she smiled and offered a hand. "Rabinia Novak, Archaeology Department, NYU."

They introduced themselves and shook hands. Rabinia Novak appeared ruthlessly practical from the waist down, clad in combat trousers and heavy work-boots, while her upper half made more concessions to style: a light blue shirt and skinny black tie, black leather waistcoat and broad-brimmed white hat, with a pair of aviator sunglasses hung around her neck completing the ensemble.

"What is it you're doing here?" said Stuart.

Rabinia gestured around them. "St Peter's Monastery. One of the earliest known Christian sites in this part of England. Founded in the seventh century by Paulinus of York – he supposedly came out here from Bernicia to bring the good word to the heathen."

Stuart grimaced at the word 'Christian' and smiled slightly at the inflection she put on 'the good word'. Apparently he still wasn't sure of Rabinia's allegiances, because his next question was "You're religious yourself, or…?"

"Christianity interests me professionally," Rabinia said. "In this country in particular. Call me an Anglophile. I mean, it's quite a story, when you think of it, how those early missionaries spread their faith."

"You sound as though you admire them," Monica said, before Stuart could speak.

"To some extent, I guess. They braved hardship and danger because of something they believed – *knew* – to be true, and convinced thousands that they were right.

And, ultimately, they created and inspired buildings, music, art, institutions, that lasted hundreds, even thousands of years. What's not to admire there?"

"But it was all a load of—" Stuart broke off as Monica trod on his foot.

Rabinia's smile stiffened. "Whether I believe it or not isn't the issue. Fact is, it seems to take big ideas – stories, narratives, call them what you like – for people to act outside their own selfish interests. These people *knew* there was a God, and what He wanted of them, so they did it."

"And gave us the Crusades and the Inquisition."

"Oh, for—" Rabinia broke off, catching Monica's eye. "The men who lived here weren't like that," she said. "They farmed, brewed mead, tended the sick – and, incidentally, they preserved knowledge in manuscripts. Frankly, I couldn't give a shit if they did that for Jesus, Buddha or Ludwig fucking Beethoven. Point is, they did it." She eyed one of her workers. "Ack – students! If you'll excuse me." She nodded to Monica and strode away.

"Weird bloody woman," muttered Stuart. Monica would have liked to have studied the site a little longer: what remained was mostly foundations, but she could make out what she thought was part of the main building's outline, and that of a circular structure that might have been the base of a tower. But Stuart was already going, so, with a last backward glance at Rabinia, Monica followed.

"She was okay," she said as they walked along the eastern shore. "Bit passionate, maybe, but it's what she cares about."

"Just wish people'd stop making excuses for religion." Stuart kicked at a pebble; after a moment, he held out his hand. Monica took it, and they continued walking in companionable silence.

Roughly halfway through the journey, Monica put a hand to her mouth. "God," she said, "that *stinks*."

"Wasn't me."

"Very funny."

"The sewage plant?"

"Other side of the island," Monica said. The breeze on her face stiffened; ghost-trails of pale sand snaked towards them. "Wind's blowing the wrong way, too." And, though noxious, it wasn't that kind of smell; it was, somehow, vaguely marine, but like nothing Monica had encountered.

"Don't know what, then," Stuart said. Despite the breeze, the smell was getting worse. "Something out to sea, maybe?"

The day had grown colder, the sun no longer so bright or warm. Monica stopped to fasten up her coat; when she looked up, she saw the sky clouding. The wind whipped hard across the beach; whitecaps striated the dun-grey water, then faded as it flattened out again. Then she saw that the horizon had disappeared: in its place was a cottony blur of grimy white, moving in from the sea.

"Shit," said Stuart. "Fog." He grabbed her arm. "The ferry."

They broke into a run, but long before they reached the bay, the fog had engulfed them, forcing them to slow down. The island's foghorn had begun to sound, a low, booming blare.

The air was burning cold to breathe now, clinging and wet. The landing stage itself was a dark blur; at first, Monica thought the boat had gone, but then she made its shape out.

"Thank goodness," she muttered; thanking God might not have been the best choice of words just now. In any case, a part of her no longer felt quite so certain no-one was listening.

They made for the boat, but a smaller black blur advanced through the mist. A couple more steps, and Monica saw it was the ferryman, and that he was shaking his head.

There was no way off Rainey save by boat, and neither the ferryman nor anyone else on the island would even consider setting off before the weather changed. Until the fog lifted, they were marooned.

Luckily, there was accommodation available at the Commodore's Rest, although if it matched the standard of the cuisine, luck was a relative term. They'd ended up having a pub lunch after all, and it had been every inch the experience they'd dreaded; forcing down the Commodore's scampi and chips proved to be a pitched battle between sheer hunger and the gag reflex. Afterwards they both felt mildly sick, and ventured outside in search of something resembling fresh air.

The fog was so thick that visibility was down to five or six feet. Monica thought it was an improvement; it gave the settings an air of mystery, at least.

Their footsteps crunched on the shingle, rang and

echoed in the mist. The foghorn blared. They walked in silence, apart, till Stuart finally said: "I'm sorry."

"What for?"

"This."

"You single-handedly caused the fog? Bloody hell, hubs."

Stuart laughed, then took her hand and kissed her. "I meant, getting us stuck here."

"You didn't know this would happen."

"Still my idea, and I wish I hadn't bothered. Place is a shithole." He grimaced. "Christ. Stinks like one, too."

The odour they'd encountered before had returned, stronger than before. "Oh, bloody hell," said Monica; for a moment, the recently-consumed scampi seemed to be considering a return to the outside world. Again, though, she noted that the stench had nothing of the sewer about it. If she'd had to put her impressions into words, Monica would have guessed at something from the very, very deep sea.

"We wouldn't have known if we hadn't come," she said. "Can't be helped now."

"I suppose." He took her hands in his. "What would you like to do, now we're stuck here? Out of the admittedly limited options?"

Neither of them were in any great hurry to return to the Commodore's Rest. Their room there was of a piece with the pub as a whole – cheap, poor-quality and (hopefully not literally, in the scampi's case) long past its use-by date. Even the foggy beach, now unseasonably cold, was an appealing alternative. Best to keep active, Monica thought; their best chance of falling asleep in that room was if they were both worn out. But they already knew how little there was to do on Rainey, and thanks to the fog there was even less. She didn't even want to contemplate what would happen if the fog didn't lift and forced them to spend another night here.

"Why don't we head up that way?" She pointed northward. "Have another look at the monastery?"

"Huh," Stuart grunted, "and run into that old battleaxe, Novak."

"She wasn't an old battleaxe," Monica laughed. "You've just got your nose out of joint because she wouldn't take any crap from you."

"I just said what I thought."

"Oh, shut up." She took his hand. "Come on, you."

It was something to do, but Monica found she was genuinely interested in seeing what remained of the monastery; Rabinia's enthusiasm for the subject must have rubbed off on her. She realised she was hoping to encounter Rabinia herself, too. She'd probably be at the site; no way she'd let a little fog stop work.

As they walked towards the headland, Monica became aware of a faint dull clanging that seemed to grow louder and richer as they neared their destination, ringing out between the low booming cries of the foghorn in the distance. Both the island's churches were in the village behind them, but the sound of the bells – distorted though it might be by the fog – was indisputably coming from up ahead. The only likely source of the sound was the monastery site; the bells certainly had an ecclesiastical sound to them.

By the time the headland's dunes came into view,

Monica was as certain of seeing Rabinia again as she was of seeing the ruins themselves, but in the event neither were visible. The riven dunes were shrouded in tarpaulins that flapped and rustled in the breeze, revealing only the odd teasing glimpse of the uncovered stonework.

By then, the bells had reached an almost painful crescendo, so much so that it was as though she was standing next to them as they rang; Monica's head, in fact, had begun to throb. Within a minute of their arrival, however – all while Monica cast about, trying in vain to identify the source of the sound – they'd died away to nothing, and all she could hear was the soft breathing rush of the sea on the shingle beach, the blare of the foghorn and the cry of far-off gulls.

"So much for St Peter," said Stuart.

Was there a dig there? If so, Monica wasn't rising to it. "Weird about those bells," she said. "Sounded like they were coming from here, but it must have been one of the churches in town. Fog must have made them echo or something."

She waited for Stuart to offer some sort of explanation, most likely something he'd half-remembered from Wikipedia, but he didn't say anything. Monica turned and found him looking at her with a slightly worried frown.

"What bells?" he said.

They went back to the Commodore's Rest for a drink; Stuart pronounced the house ale to be 'passable', while

Monica sipped less than half a glass of the vinegary house white. There was only so long they could sit around the bar, near-unpopulated as it was save for a couple of sullen-looking fishermen and the landlord morosely polishing his glasses, so they made their way up to their room.

There wasn't much more to do there, however; neither of them had brought a book along with them – Stuart had his tablet, but had no time for e-readers, while Monica still preferred an old-fashioned clamshell mobile to a smartphone. The Commodore's Rest had no wifi; the bookcase on the landing was stuffed with thrillers from the 1970s, Mills and Boon romances and Readers' Digest Condensed Books. Cooped up in the room with nothing to do, it wasn't long before boredom set in; with no better options to hand, they raided the shelves and sat in silence, reading.

The silence quickly grew oppressive; every sigh or rustling page seemed both startlingly loud, and to hold some hidden, hostile meaning. When Stuart let out a short, loud breath through his nose, Monica's first reaction was to wonder whether it was an expression of annoyance with her. That was annoying in itself – if either of them had grounds for ill-feeling towards the other, surely it was her. Stuart had been the one who'd insisted on visiting this Godforsaken place. Perhaps that was why he was irritated; he was on edge, expecting at any moment to be berated.

Or perhaps he'd just breathed out through his nose, and that was all. Even Freud had admitted that sometimes a cigar was just a cigar.

Stuart lay on the bed to read, while Monica occupied a high-backed chair beside the window. The bay and landing stage were obscured by mist, within which livid orange nimbuses of streetlight glowed even though it was still day. There was nothing to be seen or done, and it wasn't even late – seven o'clock, at most.

Monica marked her place in her book and laid it on the windowsill, then took off her reading glasses and placed them on top. Stuart, deep in glum contemplation of his own book, noticed neither this nor her approach to the bed, until the mattress shifted when she climbed aboard.

They kissed and undressed, and made love with the curtains open; any would-be voyeurs would need advanced surveillance technology to see anything through that fog, unless the landlord had wired the room for vision and sound, in which case the curtains would be neither here nor there. The idea was pathetic and absurd, but somehow oddly arousing, too, which was useful; even though she'd initiated the sex, it felt like going through the motions, and she had to close her eyes and imagine scenarios both more exotic and erotic than the current one in order to achieve release.

If Stuart realised any of that, he gave no sign; certainly he seemed to derive as much pleasure from the act as always. Perhaps he was faking, too, but Monica doubted it; Stuart's total lack of guile was part of his charm.

Afterwards, he rolled onto his side; a minute or so later, he began to snore. It always happened. Monica didn't mind; the sex had been a welcome distraction, and one of them being asleep would ease the atmosphere in the room.

But the surroundings were still claustrophobic, and Monica herself still couldn't rest. Even the fogbound shore seemed more appealing. Slipping quietly off the bed, she dressed, tiptoed to the door and let herself out.

A light breeze came in off the sea as Monica walked towards the headland again; not enough to disperse or even thin the fog, but at least it lessened the stench a little.

The dig was still deserted. The tarps over the ruins shone wetly, and crackled in the wind. Monica glimpsed stonework here and there, and went closer, reaching hesitantly out. The tarpaulins clearly weren't meant to be touched, but she wanted, very much, to see the remains of the monastery.

As she reached out, the breeze dropped, and seconds later the stench returned in full strength. As it did, the bells clanged again. Monica covered her ears; the volume was such that it was, again, as though she were standing next to them. The bells pealed out for two or three minutes before dying away as quickly as they had come. The foghorn sounded again in the returning hush; it must have done so several times in the past few minutes, she realised, but the bells had drowned it out.

A section of tarp had come loose; Monica reached out to touch it, but a voice called "Hey!" She jumped, tripped and nearly fell.

A thin figure strode out of the fog, fists clenched, then stopped and stared at her. "Mrs…" Rabinia trailed off, tried to remember Monica's married name and clearly failed. "Monica, right?"

"Hello," Monica said.

"Hell are you doing here?"

"Wanted a walk."

"This isn't exactly a beauty spot."

"You're here."

"I got this to look after." Rabinia nodded to the ruins. "Dug this shit out of a heap of sand – last thing I need's to have to dig it out again. We've been lucky till now, with the weather. Rains a lot here."

A little humour might lighten the mood, thought Monica. "Hence the name, I suppose."

"Huh?"

"Rainey?"

Rabinia crouched to adjust the loose piece of tarp. "Common misconception. The *-ey* suffix means 'island', while—"

"In what language? Celtic?"

"Think you mean Cymric, but no. Try Norse."

"Vikings?"

"They raided up and down the northern coasts pretty much at will from the ninth century on, lady – settled here, too. Left their traces behind in the language."

"So what does the 'rain' part mean, then?"

"Part of a name," said Rabinia. "Ragnar's Island."

"Who was Ragnar? Viking chief or something?"

"That's the guy."

Monica nodded at the ruins. "Did he do this, then?"

Rabinia rolled her eyes and shook her head. "No," she said, as if Monica were one of her denser students, "that was Henry VIII. This place outlasted the Vikings and the Norman Conquests too, just to get shut down by a syphilitic asshat. Ragnar *did* come here to plunder, but he ended up getting converted instead."

"As you do," said Monica, feeling the quip fall flat even as it escaped from her lips. Stop making jokes, she told herself; they were only making her look foolish in front of Rabinia, which she realised she really didn't want. The breeze had picked up; now it died again, and the smell returned in full force. "What happened?" Monica asked, putting a hand to her mouth.

Rabinia did not appear to notice the smell. "Details are a tad sketchy. Some kind of miracle, I gather. He had a revelation. That kind of thing."

There was a sound like an indrawn breath, then, from behind Monica, a wet heavy slap; it took her a few seconds to realise that a large wave had just hit Rainey's shoreline. A soft hissing sound followed as the gravid, oily water slithered back down the beach into the sea; the stench washed over the headland, stronger than ever and as it did the bells, once more, began to ring.

Monica put her hands over her ears and looked at Rabinia, to see that the other woman had done the same. Rabinia raised her eyebrows on seeing Monica, then mouthed 'this way' before heading inland, head down. Monica followed, and the two of them stumbled across an uneven ragged field until the bells had receded.

"You heard them too," Rabinia said.

Monica nodded; the same words had been on her lips. After the first time she'd heard the bells, she'd attempted to broach the subject, tentatively, with the landlord and the bar's two patrons, only to be met with looks as blank and baffled as Stuart's had been.

"I didn't think anyone else could hear," she said. "I thought I was hallucinating." Or going mad, she did not say.

"Most don't," said Rabinia. "You're staying at the Commodore's?"

"Yes."

"Me too." Rabinia shrugged. "There isn't anywhere else. Well, my students are all under canvas a little to the south of here and they seem happy enough, but they're young, dumb, and full of come. When you get older, a warm bed, a roof and a flushing toilet matter a hell of a lot more than the chance of exchanging bodily fluids."

Monica laughed. After a moment, Rabinia smiled. When the bells died away, they trudged back to the beach and plodded along the shore. The stench was still overpowering, but had diminished slightly, having reached its nadir after the big wave.

The shoreline hissed and frothed: a boundary of scum and detritus. There was the usual assortment of reeds and driftwood, rusting cans, plastic bottles, but other items were washing ashore; Monica saw crabs and an assortment of fish among them, along with other creatures entirely beyond her ability to classify. All seemed crushed or ruptured in some way, as if caught up in some vast upheaval.

They walked in silence back towards the Commodore's Rest, accompanied only by the sound of the waves and the steady pulse of the foghorn; even if they'd spoken, Monica suspected, neither would have mentioned the bells.

❖

Stuart had shifted position, but as far as she could tell he'd slept through her absence. If he *had* noticed it, he didn't say anything when she woke him for a late supper.

The Commodore's evening bill of fare – some kind of stew – was, at least, an improvement on the lunchtime one, not that *that* was saying much. It tasted reasonable enough, even though it had been simmered so long it was impossible to guess which animal or even species the meat came from (and probably better not to try.) The 'passable' beer was a help in that respect; Monica preferred wine as a rule, but couldn't have faced another glass of that house white.

"Everything okay, love?" Stuart asked, reaching out to touch her hand.

"Fine," she said, and smiled; but the word felt short and clipped, the smile insincere. She squeezed his hand, but that too felt forced. She was beginning to see him, after a decade and a half of marriage and so much else, as shallow, something she'd never perceived him as before. But he had become so hermetically sealed into his convictions, it'd become a comfort zone from which he derided all outside his experience.

It would pass, she hoped – after all, every marriage had its ups and downs, and no couple on earth could completely avoid periods of boredom with one another, if not actual dislike. She knew, too, the cause of her discontent; Stuart's atheism, which for so long she'd shared – and which she'd allowed to form her world's perimeter and boundaries – now felt reductive and restrictive, a wilful shutting off of perception.

Perhaps it was just an irrationalist tantrum, a

reaction against middle age, intimations of mortality and a world looking more doomed by the day. Part of her hoped so.

Footsteps sounded, and Rabinia appeared, crossing the floor to a small table for one in a corner by the window. She wore trainers – *sneakers*, she'd have probably said – jeans and a cashmere sweater. She gave Monica a curt nod; Monica, less curtly, nodded back.

Stuart glanced from Rabinia to Monica; Monica met his gaze and gave a hopefully reassuring smile, squeezing his hand, stroking the knuckles with her thumb. He smiled back. If he wanted a romantic dinner for two, she'd give him one, while she still could.

As the barmaid – looking almost existentially weary – approached with their desserts, thunder growled outside. The bar went still, everyone listening for the patter of rain. But all they heard was the horn, reminding them of their isolation.

That, at least, was all anyone else in the bar heard. For Monica, the rising peal of bells, distant at first, grew deafeningly loud. She winced and put her hands to her ears.

"Darling?" Stuart touched her hand again.

"I'm okay," she said. "Bit of a headache, that's all."

"Not surprised in this place."

"Got any paracetamol?"

"Sure." Stuart fumbled in his pockets; the bells, while still ringing, were no longer quite as loud. Monica saw Rabinia frowning, more deeply than Stuart: she looked not only puzzled, but somehow hurt, even angry. She'd guessed what Monica had heard, but had heard nothing herself: this particular carol of the bells had been Monica's alone.

Monica lay awake in the dark, muggy night, trying not to hate Stuart as he snored beside her. Under other circumstances she might have slept soundly too. The foghorn's steady booming cry, repeated at clock-regular intervals, was actually quite soothing; on its own, it probably would have lulled her to sleep. But Monica could still hear the bells; they hadn't stopped and rang, as far as she could tell, without any kind of rhythm, rhyme or reason, while their volume rose and fell with similar randomness. They made it impossible to sleep, or (increasingly) to entertain any feelings of warmth or affection towards those who could still do so.

Monica couldn't recall wanting anything so badly as she wanted to leave Rainey, but the fog outside the window was as thick as ever, a solid wall of murky off-white. They'd kept telling themselves that they'd only have to spend a single night on the island, but the fog seemed thicker than ever. She couldn't believe it would be gone in the morning, or the next, or the one after that. The prospect, as terrible as it was absurd, of being stranded on the island forever, confined by the never-lifting fog, suddenly seemed plausible.

She did her best to smile at the idea, but couldn't quite; rationally she knew that the fog must lift, but an amorphous sense of dread had settled on her earlier in the evening and refused to shift, a free-floating unease that battened onto anything it could find as a potential cause.

The strangest thing was that alongside the dread was a growing sense of excitement, as though she were on the cusp of some experience both terrifying and glorious.

Despite the hour, therefore, Monica was fully awake – in fact, outright restless. When the headache she'd lied about before became a dully nagging reality, the room finally grew too small. Leaving Stuart snoring peacefully, she dressed and, walking boots in hand, tip-toed to the door again.

Going outside did little to ease the headache: Monica had thought she was acclimatised to the stench, but it was now so thick and strong she could barely breathe without retching. She pressed her shirt-sleeve over her nose and mouth, but it didn't do much good as she walked up the shore-path.

The loud wet slap and hiss of a wave sounded again, followed by a second and then a third. They were becoming both louder and more frequent, although the fog wall remained immobile.

The bells, she realised, were getting louder too – louder, and faster, with an urgency that bordered on desperation. The nameless sense of panic was rising to a crescendo.

"Something's coming," she heard herself say. She didn't know why she'd said it, but no sooner had she done so than she knew it was true. The bells, as before, were coming from the headland. Had the monastery had bells like that in Viking days, and had they been a warning to flee, or a call to arms?

Tonight, at least, they were a summons; again, Monica had no rational basis for that conclusion, but was certain of it nonetheless. Without knowing why, she began running towards the dunes.

By the time Monica reached the headland, the bells' clamour had blurred into one discordant note, and wave after wave was crashing on the shore beyond the mist. The wind had picked up; gritty spume whipped her across the face. The same wind had torn the tarpaulins from their moorings: a couple flapped and crackled like flags, and Monica glimpsed one fly away through the air, but the rest were nowhere in sight. One of the toilets toppled over with a sudden crash.

The riven, gutted sand dunes were laid open to expose the monastery's remains. Monica could see the main building's foundations, some outbuildings, but the tower now stood high above the marram-grassed dune that housed it. Over the combined sounds of the bells, waves and wind, Monica now made out a low, steady chanting that, like the bells, emanated from the tower.

As she did, the bells at last abated: one by one they slowed and fell silent, until a single one remained, beginning a slow funereal toll as the waves continued to crash against the shore.

Monica strode towards the tower; it seemed very clear, now, what she must do, where she must go. It was a rare sensation, to know exactly what the right thing was and how to go about it.

As she entered the tower and climbed the winding

steps towards the uppermost level, she could still hear the last bell tolling and the voices chanting, although she saw nothing and no-one. At the top of the stairs was a window in the shape of a cross, facing north towards the open sea. At first she only saw the fog, but as Monica looked out through the cruciform window it divided, rolling back on either side of the tower to reveal an open passage leading out across the water.

Although long and wide, the passage was far from clear, because something was wading down it, hunched over in the sea. Its distance and therefore its size were hard to estimate, but Monica was sure it couldn't have been less than a hundred feet tall. It was vaguely humanoid in shape, but, even disregarding its size, it was plainly anything but human. Its body, legs and head looked bulbous and swaddled, except for what were either two long, thin forelimbs or a pair of crutches it was leaning on.

There was a dark aperture at the head that might have been a gap in the swaddling or an elongated, lamprey-like mouth – she couldn't tell if the swaddling was the thing's clothing or its skin, and those ambiguities could only be resolved by a far closer inspection than Monica had any intention of taking part in. The most important thing about it, she already knew: it was emerging from the sea – *de profundis, Domine* – and would very soon reach the island.

Monica heard what sounded like a vast exhalation, and the stench she'd encountered previously filled the tower, at its greatest strength yet; she avoided vomiting only by great effort.

The thing shuffled closer on thick, clumsy hind legs, thin forelimbs stabbing down into the water; a glistening bow wave rose around it and flopped towards the island.

The chanting continued, punctuated by the bell. Both now kept to a strict, disciplined rhythm; around her, beside her, behind, above. The sound filled her: the shape in the water continued to advance.

Afterwards, Monica was unable to recall a single word of the chant, although she suspected it may have been at least partly in Latin. At the time, however, whatever words comprised it came easily, and she found herself repeating them – first in a halting, unconfident murmur, then more forcefully, finally singing them out across the water.

She was never sure how long she'd been doing so before she realised that the thing from the sea had stopped its advance. It was hunched further forward now, over those stick-like forelimbs, which it had driven deep into the water as if to anchor it in place. It looked as though it was fighting a powerful wind; the impression was enhanced by the way the fogbank began to visibly retract from the island, albeit far more slowly than it should have. It was as if some countervailing force was trying to push the fog back towards the shore.

Monica continued to chant, and the huge swaddled shape took a shambling step backwards. As it did – and as the fogbank was pushed away from Rainey – the walls of the passage through the fog began to quiver and blur; white mist spilled into the passage, to cloak and obscure the occupant.

The huge figure staggered, flailing, struggling not to

fall. The aperture in its cowled face stretched further open and the roar that came from it made the tower shake; Monica continued to chant, accompanied now only by the bell.

The mist seemed to cling to the shape like enormous, stifling cobwebs. It struggled and bellowed, as more and more of the fog collapsed in on it. Monica caught a last glimpse of it blundering backwards, and then the fog drowned the sight before billowing away across the waters. The shape was gone: the deep waters had covered it, and it had sunk to the depths like a stone. The bell died away, leaving the monastery ruins silent; the foghorn sounded one last time. Within minutes, the sea was clear, and it had begun to rain.

"Be setting off in about an hour," said the ferryman. "Plenty of time for a last potter about."

"We'll be back on time," said Stuart.

"No problem, mate – I'll wait up for you if you're not."

"Thanks!"

"No problem," the ferryman said again. He grinned. "It's a nice day."

They walked along the shore to the castle ruins, poked around in the shops – they even climbed up Dog Fell again, where the view, Monica had to admit, seemed a little more prepossessing. Now they were leaving Rainey, the place had a little more appeal – although more to Stuart than to Monica. She was as yet uncertain exactly what, if anything, she'd gained on the island, and it was still too early to tell what she might have lost.

Stuart took her hand as they walked down Dog Fell; she squeezed back, but was still aware of the gulf between them. The sense of it hadn't lessened, not for her; she suspected Stuart remained blissfully oblivious to it all. She could, of course, never even attempt to discuss what had happened with him. Stuart would be unable to understand it, or deal with it in any way other than wholesale dismissal – either by quarrying out rational explanations, no matter how difficult to find, or categorising the whole experience as born of dream, hallucination or outright delusion on her part. She might tolerate that if she could likewise dismiss it to herself, but she never would. For better or for worse, last night's events had been real; Monica knew this with a conviction she couldn't recall ever having experienced before. And whatever it had been, it would always lie between the two of them.

They found themselves strolling towards the headland with time to spare; Monica would have been hard put to find a reason to avoid it.

In the event, the site, even though stripped of its tarpaulins, seemed undamaged. Rabinia and her students were hard at work setting things to rights: on seeing Monica and Stuart, she acknowledged them with a rather surly nod, but didn't approach.

"Some people are just bloody weird," Stuart opined, before turning his gaze to the portable toilets. The fallen one had now been righted: as with the excavation, Rabinia's team had worked hard to eradicate all traces of the storm damage. "Think anyone would mind if I..."

"I'm sure they wouldn't," said Monica, and watched

him amble off. When the toilet door had shut behind him she turned, to find herself face to face with Rabinia. "Jesus."

"Hardly," said Rabinia with a crooked smile. "You're going, then?"

Monica nodded. Rabinia looked towards the toilet block, then back to her; she opened her mouth and seemed about to ask something, then shrugged. "Fair enough," she said; her face wore the same bitter, crushed expression it had the night before in the pub. "Safe journey home." She turned to go, then turned back and held something out to Monica. "Found this in the dig," she said. "Thought you might like a keepsake." She cleared her throat. "From the workmanship, it's probably Viking."

Monica turned the small, pitted metal cross over in her hands. "Thank you."

Rabinia shrugged. "Not that you need it to remind you, though, right?"

"No."

Rabinia nodded; behind her, Monica heard the toilet door slam shut again, and tucked the crucifix into a pocket.

"Least I heard them too." Rabinia might have been murmuring so as not to be overheard by Stuart, or perhaps she was speaking only to herself. "That's something."

She turned away; this time she didn't look back. "Good work, Stefan," Monica heard her call. "Keep it up."

Stuart took Monica's hand. "Decided she was talking to you in the end, did she?" When Monica didn't answer, he sighed. "Come on," he said. "Let's get off this bloody island."

They walked back to the jetty and boarded the ferry, watching the low green-brown hump of Rainey shrink away. Sea-birds had cleared the waters of the dead, and the last traces of the red tide were fading, like a wound washed almost clean.

The Loved One

Paul Meloy

I walk my dog down to the beach every morning. I let him off the lead and sit on the remains of an old wooden groyne and watch him run. He tears into the water, bites at the low, frothing waves, and comes back panting, soaked, laughing the way only Staffs can. He's a lazy bastard, is Sid, and that's it for him, job done. I don't bring a ball because he doesn't want to chase anything. He sits by my feet and dries off while I look out to sea.

There is a coffee shop on the promenade but it's shut now. It's autumn and everything is seasonal here. In the summer I buy myself a cappuccino and get Sid a croissant. He loves croissants. They go down in one, like huge, curled grubs down the neck of a baby bird. When Sid yawns I think he resembles a baby bird, the way his whole face unhinges to reveal nothing but throat.

It's a beautiful morning. The sun isn't up yet and the moon is a rice-paper disc in the pale blue sky. I like to watch the sunrise. I try to get down here before anyone else is up so I can watch the world come alive. I'll walk Sid along the coast for a couple of hours, much to his disgust even at our gentle pace, and return as the shop is opening to get our breakfast. Sometimes there's a tanker or a container ship out on the horizon, Lego blocks pink and gold in the light of the early sun, and I give them a wave. Sid cocks his head, looking up at me with his small brown eyes, wondering, perhaps, how he ended up with an owner like me.

We've been coming down here for the last couple of years. I used to work in a nursing home and the shifts weren't conducive to any kind of routine. Before I retired I bought Sid from one of my colleagues who bred Staffs as a secondary income. She brought him in and put that pup in my arms and that was it. I'd always wanted a dog, but didn't think it was fair to leave one at home all day while I did odd hours. Now I had time to enjoy it. I have to say, though, it wasn't all fun. It took me a while to get used to the damage; as of now, he's had a mobile phone, my wallet, a couple of rugs, my spare specs, most of the lino in the kitchen and a TV remote control. I used to have a nice little decked patio area out the back of my cottage. I had one of those clay chimeneas, a small blue one, that I liked to light a kindling fire in on late summer evenings. I'd sit out in my garden chair and smoke a few cigars and have a beer. Well, Sid had my chimenea over, rooting about. Smashed it. Also, I can't sit out there anymore because it reeks of his wee where it's soaked into the wood, and his poo gets in the ruts and goes hard where I can't get it all. So it's now become a glorified dog pen.

I don't mind though – Sid's a good one. We're a proper couple. He's calmed down a lot since he had his nuts off.

I found the last few years at work dragged. I had put away a good pension and so I was able to retire a bit early, but where's the enjoyment of a lonely retirement? Before my wife passed away four years ago that was one of the things we discussed. "Get a dog," she said.

We didn't have children. Not because of any tragic biological deficits, but simply because we were both in our forties when we met and neither of us had had any long-term or meaningful relationships before then. Jenny was a pharmacist and had enjoyed a good career, and I was a hard-working bachelor who liked my own company.

We met when Jenny brought her mum into our home to have a look around. Our manager was on a course and I was supervisor for the shift, so it was my job to do the hosting. By the time I'd shown Jenny and her mum the top floor, we both knew we'd hit it off. The old girl was shot to pieces, and unwittingly prophetic when she referred to me as Jenny's husband. Jenny blushed, pretty as a picture, and that was when I noticed she had no wedding ring.

I think I made a bad joke, and Jenny blushed all the more. The rest, as they say, is history. We had a happy little marriage.

Now it's just Sid and me. We fill our days.

We were on our way back home, coming up to the slope that joined the promenade after a shorter-than-usual stroll along the beach. I was feeling a bit short of breath, and Sid was restless, nipping at my heels and barking like he was bollocking me about something. I clipped his lead on and made to drag him up the slope.

"You're a pain in my arse, Sidney," I said. He was probably hungry. I'd forgotten to bring a pocketful of snacks this morning. I usually have a selection already stashed in my coat but I remembered giving him extra yesterday because he'd had such a good turnout on the way home, filling two whole poo bags, that I'd rewarded him handsomely for not saving it up for my decking.

It was still early. The sun was up now and the thin layer of clouds above the horizon was a gorgeous, intoxicating pink. I checked my watch – it was nearly eight o'clock and still very quiet. Hardly any traffic on the coast road. Usually it was busy by now with commuters setting off for a day's grind. I could see the top of a lorry as it drove past; it was one of those old types, with grubby sheets of fabric belted along its sides. It stopped at the kerb not far above where I was standing and I heard someone get out. The cab door slammed shut with a loud, resounding bang. Sid sniffed the air and his tail began to wag.

"Lorry full of meat?" I enquired of him.

I turned to take one last look at the sea and that was when I saw the paddle boarder.

It looked like a lot of hard work to me, that paddle boarding lark. I'd watched it grow in popularity over the last few years. Boards the size of canoes and all that standing up, paddling about with a big oar. It always looked a bit aimless to me. Maybe that was the point.

I decided to stroll back down to the shore. I was in no rush to get home and Sid seemed interested in the boarder, too. He pulled on his lead and I let him tow me back onto the beach.

The boarder might have been about half a mile out, although it was hard to tell. There was nothing else visible in the bay to act as a marker this morning, no boats, no tankers on the horizon. Just him and us. I stopped a few yards from the almost flat, unhurried low tide and shaded my eyes as I looked out.

The paddle boarder seemed to notice me, too. He stopped paddling and stood still on his board. I squinted; the sun was bright, a silver coin rising to the east of the figure out at sea, but I could make out that he was wearing some kind of baggy grey wetsuit.

Sid stood beside me, his head erect, ears pointed forward. He seemed interested.

"You want a go on a paddle board, Sid?"

Sid made an inquiring chuffing sound, the sound he usually made when he was trying to get my attention.

The boarder appeared to be watching us. He had lifted his long paddle from the water and now held it cross-wise over his chest. All of a sudden I wanted to be away from there, a long way from the shoreline and back up by the promenade. The wet sand sucked at the soles of my feet. I did not have a good feeling at that moment. I turned my head and looked back up the beach, towards the road. It was silent. It was as if the whole road had been closed off. Well, perhaps it had. It wasn't unthinkable. I wouldn't know until I got up there. I tried to turn but the sand seemed too sticky. Sid barked, and I snatched another look at the paddle boarder.

He had moved off, pushing that long oar through the surface, driving away from the shore into deeper water.

I looked down. My feet were tangled in a thick, leathery swatch of wrack, washed up on the beach as we stood there. I stepped out of it, kicking the shiny brown belts away and into the sea. They reminded me of the fabric straps on the sides of those old lorries. What was I thinking about today?

"Come on, Sid," I said, and began to trudge back up the beach towards the front.

As we approached the slope that led up to the road I began to hear the sound of traffic again. Muffled at first, as if I had my fingers in my ears. As we reached the slope it was all back to normal. The traffic sounds were as they always were at that time in the morning, the regular sluggish clamour interspersed occasionally by a car horn or the catarrhal sound of a slipshod gear-change.

"Must have re-opened the road," I said.

I took the slope up to the pavement and stood for a second, watching the traffic. All seemed regular.

We went home.

I awoke in a terrible panic. I hadn't had night terrors like this since my wife died. Then, I recall waking, alone, heart pounding, with a terrible dread pressing in on me, convinced that I was about to die, sickeningly sad and alone. I'd wander the house, trying to contain that feeling of doom, staring at familiar objects as if attempting to ground myself in a reality that felt flimsy and sinister. Everything seemed insubstantial, unreal. It was ghastly. The only thing that took the edge off the panic was tuning the radio to a talk show. Music made things worse somehow, even more lonely. I'd sit and drink a cup of hot chocolate and stare at the radio, following the words, trying to imagine I was in the company of rational, existent people.

I scrabbled for the lamp on my bedside table,

desperate for light. Everything in the room stood stock still in the sudden illumination, and I had a horrible feeling that all my furniture had just avoided being caught getting up to no good.

I sat back against my headboard and shot glances around the room, trying to control my breathing. It was anxiety, I told myself, that's all. Nasty but not life threatening. My chest felt tight. Breathe, breathe, breathe. What if I just stopped breathing? What if my autonomic system packed up and I had to spend the rest of my life consciously breathing in and out? What if I woke up blind?

Right, that was it. I was letting the fear get the better of me. I got out of bed and put on my clothes. I went downstairs, the sight of Sid asleep on his back with his spatchcocked legs and bits on display giving me a smile despite the horrors, and I started to feel more integrated. I put the kettle on.

Sid got up and stretched, arse in the air. He tottered over to me and yawned. I fussed him and started feeling a bit better. I should really let him sleep upstairs with me but I didn't fancy sharing the bed with him, and his farts were, frankly, unendurable in a confined space.

I looked at the clock and saw it was only half past three. I hadn't been asleep that long.

I made a cup of tea and sat with the radio on, listening to a talk show, not really taking much of it in. Sid was sitting by my feet. His tail wagged, thumped the floor. We were thinking the same thing.

"Okay, Sid," I said, and went to get his lead.

We walked down to the seafront. It was very dark, the

moon hidden behind clouds too thick to allow even the smallest diffusion of its light. The front was deserted and no lights were on in any of the boarding houses or hotels. The pubs slumbered on the corners as though succumbed to their own fumes, leaning against their neighbours until forced awake and blinking at lunchtime.

Lunch seemed a long way off as Sid and I stood at the top of the slope that led down to the beach. I had been a bachelor for a long time before meeting Jenny, and it had been a pleasant, quiet life, but since meeting her, and following our brief marriage, I found it hard to eat alone again. I had enjoyed the company, and Jenny had been a good cook. I tended to snack now, and if I did make myself a meal I sat in the living room with the TV on, with Sid guarding the area around my feet for anything that went on the carpet.

I let Sid off his lead and followed him down the slope that led to the beach. He snuffled about for a bit along the bottom of the sea wall and then he stopped and looked up, his ears pricked. Before I could say anything, he took off, haring towards the incoming tide.

It was so dark all I could see of him was a white smudge. I stepped onto the beach and headed down towards the water. I could hear the long, low waves sliding in. I trod through more of that thick brown wrack, kicking it away, swearing, disliking the sensation of it snagging my feet. It was everywhere, a huge, slimy bloom of it roiling in the shallows and depositing on the beach.

Finally I reached Sid. He was standing in the shallow

tide staring out to sea, the brown weed lashing and rolling around his legs. He seemed to be hypnotised by something out on the water. I looked up.

I think I must have screamed. I stumbled backwards and fell, jarring my back as I sprawled in a pile of sodden wrack, and the echo of my shock was still bouncing back at me from the high, silent buildings along the length of the coast road.

The paddle boarder was less than twenty feet away. He was a tall, grey, cruciform shape, the paddle held across his chest in that high-wire walker position I had seen before, balancing him on his board.

I shuffled backwards, rucking weed in a thick ridge around my backside. My heart was pounding and it was hard to breathe.

I couldn't see the boarder's face. It was hidden within the hood of his baggy grey wetsuit. As I sat gasping for breath, one hand pressed against my chest to stem the huge, palpitating thuds of my heart, he lowered his paddle and began to push himself away from the shore.

I glanced at Sid. He was still standing in the weed-choked water, his tail wagging.

"Sid!" I said. "Here, boy."

Sid ignored me and continued to watch the paddle boarder as he propelled himself away. Soon he was too distant to pick out in the darkness, attaining an eerie speed as though the board hovered above rather than floated upon the water.

I got to my feet. My back hurt and the pain in my chest had radiated up into my throat. I closed my eyes and tried to calm myself, tried not to panic. Gradually the discomfort abated and I opened my eyes. Sid had trotted over and stood looking up at me, his head cocked. He sniffed my legs. They were soaked and swathed with weed. I grimaced and bent to pull it off in clumps.

I felt exhausted. I clipped Sid's lead back on and we traipsed up the beach. I wanted to be home, dry and back in bed. I'd let Sid up with me this time, I decided. Just for a bit of company.

I awoke late in the morning, and lay on my back staring at the ceiling. I felt the warm pressure of a body next to me and turned my head to see Sid lying with his head on Jenny's pillow. He was snoring.

I sat up and looked around the room. It was a small room, still cluttered with Jenny's ornaments and mementos. I couldn't part with them even though I did not share her taste at all in décor. Most of them were souvenirs collected on her many foreign holidays taken before we had met. We had only been on holiday once together, and that was our honeymoon. I'm not a traveller and when she booked the holiday, to a small, secluded fishing village called Parga Bay on the North West coast of Greece, it was the first time I had ever been on a plane.

Jenny had loved her trips abroad. She had often gone alone on a whim but had, on occasion, taken her old mum before she started to show signs of dementia.

It was a lovely honeymoon. I discovered Jenny was quite an adventurous woman in lots of ways which, as you might imagine, surprised and pleased me. Her sensual curiosity was reflected in the souvenirs she bought. Our bedroom, the hallway and our lounge were full of statues and vases displaying a full array of Greco-

Roman depictions of erotica. We didn't have a lot of visitors, but when we did play host to someone I took it upon myself to reposition or remove some of the more graphic pieces. Jenny had a thing for phalluses that had made me a little uneasy, to be honest, but I smiled now when I recalled how excited she was to discover a particularly spectacular endowment engraved on the side of a pottery bowl in a gift shop in Parga harbour. She had always promised to show me more, take me on a Hellenistic odyssey as we enjoyed getting old together. But of course it hadn't happened like that, and we had only had that one time together.

I got dressed and went downstairs, leaving the bedroom door ajar for Sid, should he ever decide to get out of his pit. I put the kettle on and sat waiting for it to boil. I had a vague memory of the events of last night but it all seemed so much like a bad dream that I was now unsure what had been real and what imaginary. I decided I had been in a bit of a fugue, distracted by loneliness and lack of sleep, and had suffered a hallucination of some kind.

I drank my tea and filled Sid's bowl with dry food, my attempt to regulate his digestion as meat seemed to make his movements... well, you can imagine. I was still trying to moderate his effects on my decking.

Sid heard the food rattle into the bowl and wandered into the kitchen. He had a sniff, seemed to shrug, and nosed his way through a few mouthfuls.

It was a dull day but he needed his exercise, and I found that I wanted to be out of the house. I couldn't seem to settle. When I was out I wanted to be home, and when I was home I wanted to be out. Must be my age – not a particularly comforting thing to contemplate. Maybe I should pack away those ornaments, clear the decks. I'd get some old boxes from Morrison's next time I was shopping.

We took our usual path down to the front. Last night's events were fading into those hard-to-grasp fragments that remain after restless dreams, like deteriorating images fluttering on old film. I was content to be out today, hoping the council had taken steps to bulldoze that unsightly wrack into piles against the beach wall.

But when we got as far as the front I could see there had been no attempt to clear the beach. I stood in a state of civic outrage and took in the sight of a shoreline almost concealed beneath countless mounds of brown and knotted weed. It stretched out of sight, in both directions. I was overcome by distaste but also by an unexpected and compelling curiosity, and it was the latter that led us down to wander ankle-deep in the damp, rubbery weed, scuffing through it like perplexed and unaccomplished beachcombers, looking for something but neither of us exactly sure what.

And then I stopped. I reached down and pulled up a hank of the stuff and turned it over in my hands. Jenny had books as well as ornaments, mostly full of pictures of ancient, broken Greco-Roman crockery and art, but she did have one about the flora and fauna of the Greek coastlines. This one *had* interested me, and I'd flicked through it many times, mostly enjoying the quality of the photography, but I now recalled one particular picture. A beach covered in a dense mat of tangled brown seaweed.

Phaeophyceae, it was called, and the event had been seen as something of an omen at the time. Shortly after the picture had been taken the area had suffered a 7.0 magnitude earthquake and the nearest villages had been reduced to rubble. This looked like the same stuff. I dropped it and wiped my hands on the seat of my trousers, wondering about climate change and tidal abnormalities.

We were alone on the beach. I assumed no one wanted to venture down here while this weed still caked everything, but there was a strange stillness in the air. I realised that there was no traffic again, and we had not seen another soul on our walk down here. Was it a Sunday? I'd lost track of the days. I was going to end up in a bloody home soon, the way I was going.

Sid was sniffing my legs again. He whined. I went to pat his head, reassure him I was fine, but I stopped short of touching him. In fact, I froze.

Sid whined again, and turned in a small circle. He licked my hand, still outstretched, the fingers stiff and unresponsive. A fear so intense had gripped me I could not move.

I realised that it wasn't Sid who was whining, it was me. A high-pitched mewl was coming from my throat. In my head I was screaming, but all I could produce was that prolonged and outlandish whimper.

Sid disappeared from my periphery. I could hear him, though, squelching away towards the sea. I clenched my teeth to stop the whine and by sheer will turned my head. It was a terrible effort. I knew now what it meant to be petrified.

The paddle boarder was there.

Sid was sitting at the edge of the water, his head cocked and his tail wagging.

The paddle boarder had reached the shore and was waiting for me.

I felt the strength return to my muscles and was able to move again. I walked through the piles of weed, careful not to get snagged and trip, and approached him.

I felt calm now. I could see his face, white and primeval, now the hood of his robe had been pulled back. The cape was grey and baggy and foul with grease. He held his paddle in hands that were thin and skeletal, and beckoned me with its blade.

Sid watched me step onto the board and his tail wagged and wagged. He was grinning, like a baby bird, the back of his throat wide and red, tongue lolling. His eyes were closed with delight.

I turned, and it was easy to stand on that board. It did not move in the water, did not pitch or yaw. It was like standing on a plank of wood, or the bottom of a boat.

The boarder stood behind me, put the blade of his paddle in the water and took us out to sea.

I awoke an eternity later. I was facing the edge of a great crimson beach. The sky was black, starless. The paddle boarder was gone.

I walked up the beach. The sand was paprika fine and red. The land was an immense vista of rock the same colour as the sand.

A woman was standing beneath a great outcrop. She was naked and beautiful, and I knew her the moment I saw her.

As I approached her I could see the outcrop hid the mouth of a large cave. There was something stirring in the mouth of the cave. Something huge and white. As I reached the woman, it emerged to meet me.

Sid had grown. He was mighty. I remembered him as a pup, that gaping mouth like a baby bird's. Now it was more like a nest of them; three of them together, all wide and dripping. I was pleased to see him.

The woman took my hands, drew me towards the opening that led down and down. Sid stepped aside, his heads panting and drooling, and let us pass.

It was warm down there.

I followed Jenny towards whatever Hellenistic adventures awaited us.

Devil's Fingers

Stephen Bacon

They left the hospital on a Thursday afternoon in early January. Grey sleet tapped against the windscreen as they negotiated the winding drive towards the exit.

The car smelt like all the other MOD vehicles that Laura had ever been in; a mixture of army-issue polish, nervous sweat and the stench of repressed masculinity. The driver had introduced himself simply as Oates. His buzzcut hair was so light he looked almost bald, and there was a pimple on the back of his neck that Laura tried hard to ignore.

She studied her husband's reflection in the glass partition. He appeared barely recognisable. Absent was his warmth and colour, the familiar mannerisms and his gregarious speech. He looked bereft. She squeezed his hand and offered him a warm smile. He gazed back at her, seemingly confused by the gesture.

They were briefly detained at the gates while their IDs were checked. A uniformed sentry cast a disinterested glance into the back of the car before waving them through.

Oates peered at the car's navigation panel. "Just sit back and relax now, ma'am. We'll have you home in an hour."

The journey seemed to pass quickly. Laura spent the time perusing the discharge documents that the doctors had provided. Her husband never spoke, just stared out of the window, seemingly unaware of where they were headed.

"Gavin..." Laura patted his forearm. "We'll have a chance to see the girls before we leave."

His lips parted, a faint frown creasing his brow. He didn't need to say anything to convey his confusion. Laura closed her eyes and leaned against him, wondering whether to ask Oates to turn around and drive them back to the Queen Alexandra. She resisted, mentally asserting that everything would be okay, that it was all to be expected after his ordeal. She leaned back and continued to read the dossier while her husband stared blankly out of the window.

The medical reports and the minutes of the official inquiry that had been provided by the hospital were also intended to support Gavin's RAF insurance claim. It was extremely detailed – most of it involving medical terminology that meant very little to Laura – but she was able to decipher much of what had happened to her husband in the nine days he was missing. The details filled in the blanks that the officials had left out. By the time they were reaching home she was simultaneously relieved and concerned by her understanding.

As soon as they were through the door the girls burst into the hallway and fussed around Gavin, who just seemed to pat them weakly and smile as if seeking reassurance. Laura's mother appeared from the kitchen clutching a tea-towel, her eyes studying Gavin with cautious hope. They moved into the living room and seated him in his armchair whilst the girls took it in turns to assail him with their excited chatter.

"Heather, Abbie – let your father have some space," said Laura's mum. "He's been through a lot. He's still very poorly."

"It's okay, mum," said Laura. "Let them say their hellos before we go. They've missed him terribly."

Laura went upstairs to pack some of the medication with which Gavin had been discharged. She removed a couple of paperback novels she'd stowed in the bag – he clearly wasn't up to reading yet – and instead tucked in his iPod and earphones. Maybe music would help him relax. She was just folding some extra clothes into the bag when there was a quiet knock at the door and her mum entered.

"How's things?" She sat beside Laura on the bed. "What did the doctors say?"

Laura shrugged. "Not much really, they just gave me a file with loads of reports. Said he might take a week or so to get used to the medication."

"He looks tired," said Elaine. "A few days of sea-air will do him the world of good."

"Hope so."

"We had so many lovely holidays there when you were little. Do you remember when dad used to build those huge sandcastles outside the front door, just so he could see your face when woke up and found them the next morning?"

Laura bathed in the memory for a few moments. "He told me the sand-fairies had built them. That they came at night and worked while we slept. I used to huddle in bed and imagine them outside in the moonlight, crafting turrets and moats with their tiny hands." She laughed, and the sound surprised her. It had been so long since she'd felt anything approximating happiness, the whole emotion felt alien.

"He's lost weight," her mum said. "Make sure you feed him up this week."

"You should have seen him when they found him. He must have put on a stone at least in the hospital. He looked like a skeleton at first."

"How can someone live for nearly two weeks without food and drink? What did they say about that?"

Laura shrugged. "Nothing really. I mean, the report said he'd managed to eat some kind of mushrooms or something. He did have a water canister. It's a miracle really, considering what happened to the others." She sighed. "God, what a shitty time we've had. Ah well, a new year now; hopefully things will start to look up."

"Hope so, love..." Her mum glanced at the bedside clock. "Listen, you'd better get off if you want to make it to the cottage before it gets dark. I've put together some tins and bits of food for you to take – bread and milk and teabags and stuff. In that box in the hall."

Ten minutes later Laura was helping Gavin into the passenger seat. He still looked bewildered. She fastened his seatbelt for him and waited while the girls took turns to kiss him and give him a huge hug. Her mother patted their heads. "Don't worry about anything." She gave Laura a kiss. "Text me when you're there. And remember the signal's patchy so you'll have to do it before you're at the end of the lane."

They drove off slowly, Laura doing her best to blink away the tears. It wasn't so much the prospect of leaving the girls again that bothered her, more the detached aura of confusion that Gavin seemed to have adopted. Was the medication affecting him that much, or had the mental trauma of his accident damaged far more than the doctors had thought? She stared into the rear-view mirror for as long as she could, watching the image of the girls and her mum grow smaller and smaller, before she turned onto the main road.

Laura had put Gavin's favourite CD on but he barely registered it, not even tapping the dashboard in time to the music like he often did.

"Gav, you know where we're going, don't you?"

He looked at her and nodded uncertainly.

"You understand where we're going? For a few days. The cottage."

"Cottage." His voice sounded hollow and remote, like it was the first time he'd heard the word.

"Shell Cottage, Gav – my mum's." She tried to keep the exasperation from her voice. "We've taken the girls there a few times."

He just stared ahead so they lapsed into silence. Laura focused her attention to the road. She'd long been accustomed to taking care of her self – being married to a member of the armed forces meant that it often felt like you were a single parent – so the distance ahead didn't faze her.

The journey was at least pleasant. Once she was out of the city, the traffic thinned. It was the first week in January and the coast road was empty, just a few lorries trundling along. The winter sun was low, stretching shadows across the fields. She put on her sunglasses and concentrated on driving. Gavin looked ahead, occasionally glancing at the odd landmark as they passed, more out of idle curiosity than with any sense of interest.

By the time they were reaching their destination the weather had changed. Wintry clouds had swept in, seeming to steal the colour from the land. Everything looked transformed. The familiar sights – in Laura's memories, usually bathed in summer sunshine – looked pale and insipid. Sleet gathered stubbornly on the bottom of the windscreen, impervious to the wipers. The lane that led down to the cottage was desolate. Usually the hedgerows would be crowding over into the path of the car like a guard of honour, at full reach due to it being the height of summer. Now the bushes looked forlorn and weak, almost huddled for safety against the dry-stone wall bordering the field. Grey puddles accentuated the potholes in the lane as the car's suspension groaned with each shuddering bump. Laura was relieved by the time the lane opened up into the clearing beside the cottage and she caught sight of the sea.

British beaches were never quite as vivid as the holiday brochures implied, but she'd always been impressed with this section of the coast; the golden sand, the unspoiled views, the beautifully spectacular cliff-top walks. However none of that was apparent now. The view was a murky grey. It was difficult to distinguish where the sea ended and the sky began. Even the beach looked barren and hazy.

"Won't be a minute." Laura climbed out the car and hurried down the steps to the cottage, which stood on an elevated man-made plateau overlooking the beach. She fumbled around with the keys for a moment before opening the front door and stepping inside. It felt cold and sparse. She went into the kitchen and flicked on the electricity and water switches. The cottage smelled of dust and winter, but beneath it lay a familiar aroma of nostalgia. Something she couldn't quite put her finger on. Maybe it was her imagination. She lit the gas fire and switched on some lamps. Already it looked far more welcoming. She drew back the net curtains from the window and peered out across the expanse of sand, her eyes following the curve of the bay. There wasn't a single person visible.

By the time she'd returned to the car she was out of breath. Gavin smiled wanly at her. She helped him out of the passenger seat and supported him as they negotiated the steps together. She could feel his clutching twig-like arms. She led him to an armchair near the fire and placed a cushion behind him. He peered around the room as if seeing it for the first time.

"We brought the girls here." Laura tried to keep the exasperation out of her voice. "Remember?"

He nodded uncertainly.

"Want the news on?" She switched on the television. The image of a smartly-dressed female newsreader appeared, the picture glitching sporadically as bursts of pixels flickered at random. "Signal's a bit crap, I think. Must be the weather."

He smiled absently. He leaned into the cushion,

resting his head against the back of the chair. He looked exhausted, his eyes half closed.

"I'll unpack, then make us some tea. Why don't you have forty winks?" She went back out to the car to fetch the case and the boxes of food.

They had a meal of spaghetti and meatballs. Instead of sitting at the table they ate it on trays on their laps, seated around the fire. Laura draped a blanket around Gavin's shoulders. He had a chill that he couldn't seem to shake off.

"I'll run you a bath. That'll warm you up."

As she waited for the bath to fill she watched him dozing in the chair. The smell of the lavender bath cream was intoxicating. Steam filled the bathroom, making the view insubstantial, unreal. Once the bath was ready she left him napping for a few minutes while she washed up the dishes in the kitchen. She glanced at the clock on the wall. It felt much later than it actually was.

She managed to get him into the bath without much trouble, the warm water acting like a tonic to his bones. She could see his face change as the heat invigorated him. It was a flicker of the Gavin she knew, a glimpse of the man she recognised as her husband. He looked so comfortable that she left him there with his eyes closed, and went into the adjoining room. She reclined on the bed and picked up the manila folder. For the next fifteen minutes she read the reports, vaguely aware of the sounds of him bathing, finding herself drawn deeper and deeper into the realities of what he had been through.

They'd been on a reconnaissance mission in the waters of the Norwegian Sea, a Royal Navy submarine with a crew of 93. According to what the military officer had told her in the hospital, HMS Dignity had officially been investigating sources of oil and natural gas on the seabed, nearly 2000 metres down. They had meant to rendezvous at a particular point but the communication channels had failed so the captain had ordered the vessel to plot a new route, diving deeper into the colder water in an effort to make up the time. Somehow the vessel had malfunctioned – the investigators' report would be forthcoming once they'd examined the data – but the fact of the matter was that the submarine had crashed in unfamiliar waters, damaging the sonar equipment and tearing a fifteen metre hole in the bow. The vessel had lain stricken and without communication, during which time the Royal Navy launched a search and recover mission.

Laura gripped the paper tightly as she read this, knowing that the Navy had not notified any of the crew's families until they'd finally discovered the location of HMS Dignity nine days later. She blinked away tears as she read the words 92 *confirmed deaths*.

There was an extensive doctor's report about Gavin's physical condition that Laura didn't entirely understand. It seemed like a string of medical terms – *musculature wastage, hypotension, koilonychia, bradycardia, depleted cognitive function, clathrus archeri*. It was clear from the reports that they were inconclusive, that the physicians did not fully agree with the findings. One had even suggested further research was required before a verdict could be given.

She heard Gavin getting out of the bath so she put the file on the bedside table and hurried to help him. He was standing on the mat with a towel wrapped around him. The sight of his emaciated body was startling as she helped him dry and dress. He appeared re-energized, his attention more focused.

"Listen why don't you have a lie down and watch the TV or something? I'm just going to have a walk up the lane and text mum – I forgot to let her know we've arrived safely, and the signal's rubbish here."

He nodded. She watched as he shuffled to the armchair and switched on the television with the remote control, resisting the urge to take over and do it for him. The TV signal was still a bit glitchy but he didn't seem to mind. His face looked bronze in the glow of the fire, the warmth of which had transformed the cottage. Laura used her phone to photograph a few of the sections of the military reports before throwing on her coat and going outside.

She sheltered beside her car and tried the phone but there was no signal, so she trudged along the lane, turning the collar of her coat against the sleety flakes that swirled in the wind. She found a spot against the hedge where her phone showed a faint signal. She quickly fired off a text to let her mum know they'd reached the cottage and were settled, before opening up the phone's internet browser and, after studying the photos she had taken, googled a few of the medical terms. She spent a fascinated ten minutes reading the entries before tucking her phone away and hurrying back to the cottage. The visibility was poor. Somewhere distant, across the black expanse of the bay, a light sparkled intermittently. It was the lighthouse on the point of the headland. Somehow the sight gave her comfort.

Gavin looked up from the TV as she entered the cottage and locked the door. She took off her coat. "It's freezing out there."

They watched TV together for a while. He was definitely more responsive now, smiling at the comedy film. She reached out and held his hand for a moment, elated at catching another glimpse of the old Gavin.

It was as they were undressing for bed that she saw it. He had removed his shirt and was in the process of slipping on his vest when she caught sight of his back in the dim lamplight. "What's that?"

"Huh?" He half-turned.

"On your shoulder. Looks like a lump." She walked round the bed and peered closely. His skin looked translucent, blue ribbon-like veins visible beneath the surface. The bones of his collar and shoulder were accentuated by the weight he'd lost. Laura pressed the lump tentatively. It might have just been the poor light but she thought the skin around it had a pinkish tinge, like it was enflamed. "Does it hurt?"

"No."

She held him then, and it occurred to her how fragile he appeared. He had always been the strong one, the driven and focused one, the one who rarely got ill or felt down. It was as if her whole world had catastrophically shifted by the seismic effect of his trauma, and she suddenly felt vulnerable and exposed. She clutched him, glancing down, seeing the shape of each of his ribs, the jut of his hip.

They climbed into bed and she switched off the bedside lamp. The room felt strangely distant, like it was a parody of her memories. Laura hugged him and listened to the night sounds – the susurration of the tide, the cry of roosting gulls, the settling creaks of the cottage. Unbidden, the question slipped out. "It must've been terrifying – in the sub, I mean?"

As soon as she'd said it she mentally kicked herself for the stupidity of the question. There was a long silence. Her arms were around him but he had his back to her so she couldn't see his face. She thought perhaps he'd drifted off to sleep, but then he spoke.

"I think I must've blacked out at first. I heard the sirens and saw the emergency lights but I was drifting in and out." He said each word carefully, as if the task was immense but it was worth the effort. "I wasn't sure where I was, whether I was upside down or facing the ceiling. I kept being sick. By then the water must've come in. I remember the cold. So cold. Wasn't sure what'd happened. It was freezing, agony at first but in a way it numbed everything. I slept. I was in the water, floating, my head close to the top. Tried to wrap my foot against something under the water, like...to anchor myself, I suppose. There was bodies floating but I was too...exhausted...to move them. Didn't want to move myself. Too shocked. Scared. I could hear a weird beeping sound and the crunching of rock or something. Must've been where we grounded..."

Laura felt herself holding her breath. She was terrified of breaking the spell. His words were building up speed, his voice becoming more like that of the old Gavin.

"No idea how long I was drifting for. In and out of sleep, I mean. I think, in the back of my mind, I kept expecting someone to come. I thought the water level would drop. It never occurred to me that it might rise...After a long time the lights went out and I was in complete darkness. Just the sounds of water splashing and the grinding against the side of the rock. All the beeps and sirens had stopped. That was the worst part then. It felt like I'd died. Or lost my mind..."

She cuddled him and kissed the back of his head.

"But I kept being sick. It must've been the water. Or the shock. The darkness was...well, I must have drifted off again because I thought I could hear kid's voices, playing hopscotch or skipping or something, I don't know...The darkness was horrible. It felt like that for a long time. Sometimes I couldn't tell whether my eyes were open or closed. It was as if I was drifting alone, I couldn't feel anything around me other than the solid console, or whatever it was that my foot was attached to. I was terrified of letting go, even though something hard was rubbing against the skin of my leg, rubbing it sore as I drifted in the water. I remember crying, part of me just wanting to go to sleep and not wake up, when I felt, in the darkness, something take my hand."

Laura closed her eyes, her head against his back. "When they rescued you?"

He swallowed audibly. "No – before that. I felt

something in my hand. It was like all my fears left. Like how a child must feel when a parent takes its hand."

"What do you mean?"

"Well, it wasn't a hand, was it? How could it have been? It was an eel. There were others, I could feel them touching me beneath the water, nudging me..."

"Ugh."

"No, it was...*comforting*, I suppose. I wasn't scared. I've no idea how they got in. In the hospital they said I must have hallucinated, it couldn't have been eels because otherwise the air pocket would've gone, if water was entering from the outside. But how did I eat those...other *things* if they didn't come in from outside?"

"What were they? The report said some kind of, like, mushroom or something."

"No idea. I felt them in the water. By then I was really weak. Kept being sick. I'd found the water canister, it was bobbing on the surface, and I kept having sips from it. The eels had gone. It's as if things came just when I needed them – eels when I was scared, the water canister when I was thirsty, the fungus thing when I was hungry... Anyway, I felt them in the water. They had stringy bits to them that caught on my fingers. I lifted one up, thinking it was a vegetable or something, and bit it. I was so weak by then I would've eaten anything. I felt better – less dizzy, had more strength. I did that for what felt like days. Every time I needed one I'd feel it in the water. Stopped me being sick."

Laura had seen pictures of the things she'd googled on her phone – the *clathrus archeri*, or octopus stinkhorn fungus – and, frankly, the notion of eating such monstrosities filled her with disgust, but the fact that he had done just that added further admiration to the horror he'd had to endure.

She suddenly realised he sounded normal, like she was in bed again with the old Gavin, and her heart lifted, and she buried her head against his back and hugged him tight. She felt him wince and half-draw away, and suddenly – remembering the swollen patch on his shoulder – the lightness in her heart vanished and the crippling fear that had plagued her for months returned.

Laura woke to the sound of gulls squabbling on the roof. She lay for a few minutes, enjoying the rare luxury of not having to attend to the girls, delaying the moment when she'd need to throw back the covers and step out into the cooler air of the bedroom. A grey light spilled from the gap between the curtains. The sound of the surf teased her with its languid murmur.

She climbed out of bed and pulled on her dressing gown. Gavin was sleeping, half uncovered, on his side. She noticed something on his back, just to the right of his spine. She bent closer and squinted at it. Needing a better view, she switched on the bedside lamp.

There was a gash about two inches long. The wound looked tender but it wasn't bleeding. She reached out to touch the area around it, but then something aroused a sensation of fear, and she paused. "Gav – wake up." She touched his bare arm lightly. "There's a cut I need to dress."

He seemed remote again this morning, as if the

familiar Gavin she'd glimpsed the previous night had been nothing but a dream. He sat on the side of the bed whilst she hunted for the first-aid box under the kitchen sink. She taped a bandage over the wound, wincing as its centre glistened. He appeared listless, distant, staring into space as she did her best not to hurt him.

"I'd better phone the doctors when we get back. That looks nasty. Can't believe they'd discharge you like that. Disgusting."

The day was a cold one, but dry and brighter. Overnight the sleet had stopped. Wind gusted around the eaves and scattered sand against the windows. The sea was a roiling mass of grey and white, froth lingering on the beach like the memory of waves. Laura and Gavin sat with the gas fire on, the coffee-table covered with the jumbled pieces of a jigsaw that Laura had found in the cupboard. The tinny radio played hits from the 1990s as static did its best to decimate the reception completely.

"The girls have missed you so much. I can't wait until you're back on your feet, back to your old self."

He smiled thinly and surveyed the jigsaw pieces.

For lunch she warmed them some tomato soup, poured into gaudy brown bowls that looked like they'd been purchased in the 70s. Afterwards they returned to the jigsaw, Laura talking about holidays they'd been on, in an effort to awaken another glimpse of the old Gavin. *Her* Gavin. He smiled affectionately when she spoke about the girls.

As the afternoon wore on she noticed his eyelids looking heavy, his face pallid and taut.

"Why don't you have a nap?"

He nodded and leaned his head against the armchair back. Laura browsed the bookshelf in the corner, selecting a Maeve Binchy from the assortment of tatty paperbacks, then took a seat in front of the window where the light was better. She read for half an hour, noticing after a while that Gavin had drifted off to sleep, his mouth open, chest rising and falling with each breath. He looked so vulnerable.

She half-turned in her chair and peered out the window. The beach was deserted. A few lights burned in the diminishing light over on the far side of the bay but otherwise it was easy to imagine they were the last two people on Earth. The thought prompted a pang of guilt and she picked up her phone to text home, but tutted at the lack of signal. She stood and quietly threw on her coat. Gavin looked peaceful enough. She ducked out the door and walked up the lane, dialling as she neared the end. Her mum answered after a few rings. Laura could hear how anxious she was, so she was quick to reassure her that everything was fine, that Gavin was making encouraging process. The girls came on the line next, a maelstrom of excitement, and Laura closed her eyes as she talked, willing herself to imagine a time very soon when their family would be back to how it was before. Tears brimmed in her eyes and she fought to keep her voice under control. Soon it was time to say goodbye and, before hanging up, she promised to call again the next day.

Darkness descended quickly. The lights in the cottage seemed that little bit too dim. Even the glow from the fire was subdued, not so much casting shadows as creating imperceptible movement in the corners of the sitting room.

By the time Gavin awoke, Laura had completed a considerable section of the jigsaw. His eyes looked sharper, his skin had more colour.

She cooked them dinner. A simple pasta dish with some tinned tuna and some dried penne that she'd found in the food box her mum had prepared. They ate in silence. Laura wanted to tell him that she'd called home, but part of her wanted him to ask, himself, whether she'd spoken to the girls. He didn't.

After dinner she washed up and left the dishes to dry whilst she ran a bath for herself. Gavin was watching the television. The inane canned laughter was at odds with his solemn expression. She went up to the bathroom, closed the door and undressed. The steam from the hot water left sinuous trails in the air, fogging the mirror and the tiny opaque window. She felt trapped, claustrophobic. She stood on the lid of the toilet and pushed open the small sash at the top, peering through the gap. It was dark but the moon was visible, silvering the waves that crashed on the beach.

A few minutes later she was in the warm embrace of the bath. She closed her eyes and allowed herself to drift.

She knew something was wrong the minute she switched off the hairdryer. She could hear a tapping sound downstairs, urgent and irregular. She tightened the belt of her dressing gown and hurried down.

Gavin was lying on the floor, arms outstretched, banging the side of the table with the flat of his hand. He grunted when he spotted her, his face changing.

She helped him to her feet, assessing whether to call for an ambulance or drive him to the hospital herself. Due to his slender frame she had little trouble helping him back into the chair. He grunted again. "I'm okay, I'm okay..."

His voice reassured her. "Gav, first thing in the morning I'm taking you back to the hospital."

"Honestly, I'm fine."

"You're *not* fine. What the hell were you doing?"

He shook his head. "Not sure, think I must've dozed off and fell..."

"I'm worried, Gav. Those wounds, your fall...You don't seem yourself."

"I'm fine."

She sighed. "Let me check that dressing, see if it needs changing." She lent him forward in the chair and lifted up his top. The dressing was dark in the centre. "Hang on, I'll fetch the bandages. It does need changing."

She opened the green box and took out the roll of bandages and surgical tape. She carefully removed the old dressing, grimacing at the brighter blood that had soaked into it. It looked like the fall had opened the wound. She dabbed away at the cut. Just as she was about to apply the new dressing, something moved in the centre of the wound. She hesitated and stared at it, horrified, angling Gavin so that his back was turned to the lamp. The wound reacted, darkening in colour. Laura blinked. She could have sworn that the darkening effect was like that of a pupil reacting to the light, constricting. She had the uncanny feeling that she was looking not at a cut in her husband's back, but at an eye.

She woke during the night, needing the toilet. She'd had a troubled few hours of sleep. The cottage felt cold. Her bedside clock cast a red glow. It was 2.47; that point when the night was at its darkest. She groped her way to the bathroom. After she'd finished, she washed her hands. The pipes rattled and gurgled as the water flowed, so cold it made her fingers ache. Somewhere nearby she heard the tank hissing as it refilled. As soon as she turned off the tap the silence felt fragile, expectant. It was then that she heard Gavin cry out.

"Gav!" She hurried into the bedroom. He was half-sitting up, wrapped in the covers. She clicked on the lamp. He looked shocked, reaching up and feeling at his shoulder.

"What is it?" She came closer at saw straight away that the lump had advanced to what looked like infection. The skin had an angry redness. She pressed the swollen area gingerly, eliciting a flinch from Gavin. The lump felt hot, the skin waxy and distended. All at once she saw something wriggle beneath, pulsing the flesh of his shoulder like a spasm. She cried out in surprise. Gavin screamed and rolled onto his side, clutching at the shoulder. There was an explosion of blood from between his fingers. Something was erupting from him. A worm-like creature, several inches long, protruded from the wound, flexing and wriggling in the air. Gavin screamed again – a desperately feral sound, unhinged and barely human. Blood poured from where he was trying to stem the wound. He arched his neck; his throat seemed to elongate to an impossible angle, bulging hideously.

From downstairs came a heavy pounding, followed by a splintering of wood. Something was coming in through the front door.

There was another explosion of blood from Gavin and the repugnant larva emerged from his shoulder, writhing on the bed. It was six inches long. Laura screamed and stepped back. The worm-like parasite twisted its body across the duvet and dropped off the side. She jumped onto the bed and tried to see where it had gone but already it had vanished, leaving a bloodstained pattern on the carpet.

Gavin was motionless. She shook him but he was unconscious. She tried to drag him off the bed but fear had sapped her strength and she panicked. The sounds downstairs were terrifying.

His stomach had been exposed where she'd tried to move him. She saw multiple lesions in his skin, tiny puckered mouths bearing sharp teeth that bit and gnawed at the air. A couple of them had rolling black tongues. She fled out of the bedroom and into the bathroom, slamming the door behind her. She threw across the bolt, her breath coming in ragged sobs. Tears splintered her view. She fumbled at her phone but knew instinctively it was of no use. With her back pressed against the door she dropped to her knees and tried her best not to make a sound.

At some point she must have passed out because she woke in the early hours of the morning, her body stiff and numb, chilled to the bone. Her head was thumping. She tried to sit up but the linoleum stuck to her skin as if it had become fused. The sky through the opaque window looked black, the moon a fragmented pale disc, agonisingly beyond reach. She managed to struggle to her feet and creep to the door, pressing her ear against the cold wood.

Whatever it was had stopped moving around out there. The silence was profound. She couldn't even hear the tide outside. She paused for a few minutes with her breath held. Nothing. Then – a clattering from downstairs. It sounded like someone was throwing things around again. She carefully slid back the bolt and turned the handle, cracking the door open an inch as she peered through the gap.

The landing was a mess. There was a pool of something black on the carpet. The wall was stained with streaks of blood. She was shivering, a pale fragile figure almost too petrified to function. She stepped forward. A creak of floorboards beneath her feet. She edged towards the top of the landing and the stairs became visible. Trails of viscera lay in clumps on the carpeted steps, some of them steaming. Something large was moving around down there. Bumps and crashes as things were overturned. A monstrous chittering sound, like nothing Laura had ever heard before.

She turned quickly into the bedroom, wary of being betrayed by the creaking floorboards. She closed the door and carefully turned the key, praying the lock mechanism was robust enough to offer some faint hope. She turned towards the bed.

What was left of Gavin was spread across the duvet. She took it all in at once, a sight almost too nightmarish to comprehend – pale skin, gore-streaked pillows, exposed ribs, staring dead eyes. His entrails had cascaded over the edge of the bed like seaweed. What remained was an empty vessel.

Her mind teetered for a moment. Despite everything, she felt unnaturally calm. From downstairs the chittering rose louder, followed seconds later by a deafening splintering of wood. It took her a few moments to realise the thing was trying to make its way up the stairs.

She leapt to the door and snatched the key away, pressing her eye to the keyhole. There was a warm trickling sensation that she half-registered as her own bladder voiding, seconds before the glistening black thing loped into view. Only then could she scream.

The Crawling Hand
Guy N. Smith

The incoming high tide sparkled in the late August sunshine, advancing on the sandy beach, wave after wave. The tall well-built man swept his shrimping net along the edge, scraping the sand, lifting it clear every few strokes with a rhythmic motion and depositing each catch in a bucket behind him. The evening promised a record haul, he thought, shaking the net so that all that remained within it was a bunch of wriggling crustaceans. He smiled his satisfaction, lifted the brim of his baseball cap and wiped the sweat from his broad forehead.

Ken Casey visited the Welsh coast several times every year, travelling from his home in the Midlands and staying in a chalet adjoining the cottage of his long-time friend Bryn Jones on the outskirts of the nearby small village. On occasions he accompanied Bryn on a sea fishing trip. One was planned for tomorrow.

The beach was deserted, there was not a soul in sight along its length. Doubtless the holiday makers from the caravan site some distance away had retired for their evening meal. That was fine by Ken, nosey parkers gathering round him and asking stupid questions were a damned nuisance.

The basket was almost full. Another couple of sweeps and he would call it a day; a meal for himself and Bryn, and maybe a sea trout or two if they were successful on the morrow, and he would take the remainder home with him.

One final sweep. God, the net was full to the brim, threatening to snap the cane handle as he lifted it clear of the water. He shook it, depositing a shower of shingle and wet sand and leaving behind a wriggling mass of shrimps.

That was when he noticed something else amongst them, something much bigger that was struggling to extricate itself. A crab? No, it wasn't a crab, the shape was all wrong and there was no shell visible. Shrimps were pushed aside and then whatever it was came into full view.

God Almighty! Ken recoiled, dropped the net so that its contents spilled out on the sand, revealing what was undoubtedly a human hand! It lay there akin to some strange creature that was puzzled by what had occurred. It should have been lifeless – the long bony fingers with ragged fingernails twitched slightly. The skin was yellowed and wizened, bone showing in places like it had started to decompose and then stopped. The wrist was jagged as though it had been crudely chopped from the arm.

It moved, those fingernails digging into the sand, twisting around, creeping towards the man who stared at it in sheer disbelief, the bile rising in his throat. It was impossible, a nightmare taking place before his very eyes on a sunlit beach.

Ken couldn't believe what he saw, sheer terror rooting him to the spot. Its very movements were threatening, like it was aware of his presence and meant him harm.

With a supreme effort, he stepped back, almost fell. Stumbling away, the net falling from his shaking hands. *Flee, flee whilst you still can.*

Somehow he made it to the rocks which bordered the beach, clawed his way up them, scraping hands and knees in his blind panic. He dared not glance behind him, afraid to set eyes on that revolting severed member which had no right to exist and to be living. There had to be some logical explanation, maybe a revolting replica that somebody had made and deposited on the shoreline as a sick joke. How it had been engineered to move was beyond him but that could be the only explanation.

Eventually, shaking in every limb, he arrived back at the chalet, his trembling fingers having difficulty inserting the key. Once inside he slammed the door shut and locked it. Then he poured a generous portion of whisky from the bottle he kept in the cupboard, gulped it down, sank into an armchair. No way would he ever go down to that beach again.

Towards dusk he heard the sound of a radio in the adjacent cottage. Bryn was home and Ken needed somebody to talk to, even if the other might think he was crazy.

Cautiously he opened the door and peered out, fearful that that hand might have followed him up here. Thankfully there was no sign of it. He breathed an audible sigh of relief and stepped outside.

"Come in." Bryn Jones answered his knock, a tall balding man and keen sea fisherman who had been born in the village and had lived there all his life. "Goodness, man, you look like you've seen a ghost. What the devil's up with you?"

"You'll think I've lost it," Ken lowered himself into the proffered chair, "but I've just got to tell somebody."

"Go on then, try me."

Falteringly Ken related the events of that evening. Even telling them was something of a trial.

"Hmm," the other nodded, showed no sign of disbelief. He lit a cigarette, blew a cloud of smoke up to the ceiling. "I've been wondering for the last few years when that severed hand would crawl out of hiding again."

"You...you've seen it then?"

"Not personally but the story goes back to the days of my great grandfather."

"Okay, tell me about it then, Bryn."

"Bear in mind that I'm only recalling legend which was passed down through my family. There was a guy named Cledwyn who lived on his own in a wooden shack, long demolished, at the other end of the village. He used to help on the fishing boats and do odd jobs for folks. Nobody liked him; most folks, especially the children, were scared of him. He was a thief and was known to have stolen from some of the villagers. Crazy, he was. Walking down the main street shouting insults at folks. These days they'd put him a looney bin, but not in those times."

Ken nodded, licking his dry lips.

"Anyway," Bryn continued, "one day he was out fishing on a boat with two or three other guys. He made the mistake of stealing from one of them, probably money. Like everybody else they'd had more than enough of him, so they grabbed hold of him and chopped one of his hands off with a cleaver, just like what used to happen to a lot of thieves in those days. They threw the hand overboard and dumped Cledwyn ashore, bleeding like a stuck pig. Somehow he survived and lived another few years. He used to stamp down the street shouting obscenities and swearing revenge. Eventually he died and was buried in an unmarked grave in the churchyard. The grave's still there, strange thing is nothing grows on it, not so much as a single weed. Even today folks keep well clear of it."

"Creepy!" Ken sensed a tingling in his spine.

"A few years later a couple of those fishermen who had chopped off Cledwyn's hand were found dead on the beach. Their throats had been ripped out!"

"Oh, my God!"

"In those days police investigations were not what they are today, a few enquiries amongst the villagers and that was that. Until around forty years or so ago when a guy who was a descendant of those two fishermen was found dead on the beach. He, too, had had his throat ripped out!"

"Oh, Jesus Christ!"

"There was another murder investigation, much more thorough this time. We were all under suspicion but eventually the cops gave up, just left the case on file. You may have read about it in the newspapers?"

"I vaguely remember it, but I wasn't coming here then, so to me it was just another murder."

"Everybody here, including myself, was getting windy. The locals avoided the beach. A couple of years ago a holiday maker reported seeing this hand but nobody believed him, except me and one or two of the older villagers. They reckon that severed hand somehow lived on in the sea and was seeking revenge for what those fishermen did to Cledwyn. Don't ask me how, I guess only the Devil himself knows."

"But why me?" Ken shook his head. "I had nothing to do with cutting off that guy's hand. But, believe me, the way that hand moved after I dumped it out of the shrimp basket it was out to get me."

"There's no answer to that," Bryn stubbed out his cigarette. "Maybe after all these years it's getting active again, wants revenge on all and sundry. Who knows."

"Can it...can it leave the beach?" Ken's voice trembled. "Get up here?"

"That we don't know." Bryn refrained from adding *until it happens.*

"Well, I'm going to sleep with that coal pick by my bed." Ken rose shakily to his feet. "Whatever, if it comes to my place I'll smash it to smithereens."

"Are you coming out on the boat with me tomorrow?"

"You bet I am. And I'll carry on having short breaks here, but the only fishing I'll do will be with you, well out at sea. I guess it'll be late Spring before I get down here again though."

❖

Lizzie Lawton was an exceedingly beautiful brunette in her late twenties. Married at 18, she had divorced a couple of years later, the reason being her infidelity to her all too mild-mannered husband. Sexual pleasure dominated her life, and it earned her good money in the Birmingham suburb where she lived.

However, from time to time she craved a break from her somewhat drab surrounds and that small Welsh seaside village appealed to her. Hence with the advent of a warm late Spring week she booked a holiday at a B&B at the same village which, unbeknownst to her, coincided with Ken Casey's first short trip of the year.

Lizzie decided upon a stroll along the deserted beach before driving into Portmadoc for a pub supper. It was very pleasant along by the incoming tide with dusk approaching.

She had almost decided to retrace her steps when something sharp and icy cold fastened around her ankle. She gave a cry of pain, lost her balance and fell headlong on to the sand.

She screamed as she saw a dismembered human hand crawling up her leg and, with remarkable speed, fastening itself onto her throat. Her cries became gurgles as she attempted in vain to free herself from her attacker.

She was dead within minutes, her body sprawled at the edge of the incoming tide, arms and legs splayed, her gaping throat gushing blood.

The hand extricated itself and with crab-like movements scuttled away. This time it did not head back into the sea, instead moving towards the rocks, beyond which lay the village and camp sites.

It was Ken's first visit of the year to the Welsh coast. He still had an uneasy feeling about the beach down below Bryn's cottage; no way would he venture down there again. Forget the shrimps, he vowed to himself, from now onwards he would concentrate on sea fishing.

"Good to see you again, Ken." Bryn emerged from his adjacent cottage, hand outstretched. "Make yourself at home and tomorrow we'll go out and see what we can catch. I had a couple of excellent trips last week."

"Any sign of that hand?"

"Not a sign. It probably won't show up again for years. If ever. I try not to think about it."

"Wish I could forget it. I know full well it meant me harm. Thank God I managed to escape. Why it should single me out is puzzling. As you told me its previous victims all had a connection with its severing from that thief's arm."

"Maybe it hates all humans because of what they did to it. You scooped it up in your shrimp net and that infuriated it. Who knows? Anyway, we'll get off to an early start tomorrow."

It was shortly after 7am when Bryn eased his boat out to sea. The day was fine and warm. "Forget that bloody hand," he reminded his companion, noting a tenseness in the other's expression. "I've fished these waters hundreds of times and I've never seen it."

"I guess you're right," Ken forced a smile. All the same

he was glad of the large sharp-bladed knife, used for gutting fish, which rested close by. If that disgusting hand should show itself then those scrawny fingers would be amputated with a single blow.

A mile from shore they cast their lines and concentrated on fishing. Over the next few hours they had a number of catches between them. Mackerel were used as bait, they were in abundance today, and within the first couple of hours one of the large baskets was full to the brim. Dogfish and tope were mainly cast back, although Bryn kept a couple of huss for his own consumption. Sea bream were collected in another wicker container.

"I think that will do for today," Bryn laid his rod on the deck, wiped his damp forehead with the back of his hand. "Not too bad a haul. I guess we'll be having mackerel for supper, and I'll drop the rest off tomorrow at a fishmonger in Portmadoc. He takes everything I can supply him with."

"It's been a great day," said Ken, a hint of relief on his face. "Maybe we can manage another trip before I go home on Wednesday."

"Sure," his companion replied. "We'll try a bit further down the coast then."

The sun was beginning to sink in the western sky as they chugged back into the small harbour. That was when they noticed a gathering some distance down on the rocky beach. Voices drifted on the breeze.

"Christ, look there!" Bryn pointed. "There's police and that's the Coastguard Land Rover parked there. Something's up for sure. Probably a swimmer or surfer got into trouble. Strange because the sea's calm enough

– not like last Christmas Day when a bloody fool was surfing out there in a rough sea and the waves bashed him up against the rocks. The stupid bugger was dead when they managed to get him out."

Ken shaded his eyes, tried to make out what was happening. "They've got a stretcher, there's somebody on it, and here comes an ambulance."

"None of our business," Bryn unloaded one of the baskets. "We'll have to carry these up to my place between us. Then I'll cook us a mackerel supper if you'd like to join me."

"Fine. I'll go and change as soon as we've carted this lot up there."

As Ken unlocked the cabin door he noticed some deep scratches on the woodwork, from ground level up to the handle. Christ, what had made that mess? As he depressed the handle he was aware that it was wet and sticky. He snatched his hand away and in the waning daylight saw dark red streaks that were icy cold.

Blood! He recoiled, stared in horror and disbelief, glancing about him in sudden fear. He peered all around him as visions of that grisly severed hand returned. But there was nothing in sight. There had to be a logical explanation, although right now he could not think of one. *Pull yourself together, your imagination's running riot.* Maybe a holiday maker had cut their hand and was looking for somebody who could give them a bandage.

He stepped inside, slamming and locking the door behind him. Then he rushed to the sink, swilled his bloodied hand, tried not to look. He was shaking uncontrollably. Maybe Bryn could offer an explanation.

"Strange," Bryn served mackerel on to a couple of plates, doing his best to make light of the recent happening. "I'd say it was a dog. There's one or two that roam the village, bloody nuisance they are, scrounging any scraps they can find. One probably scented food in the cabin, scratched the door trying to get in."

"That doesn't explain the blood on the handle."

Bryn hesitated. "It could well have cut its paw on something, maybe it had got a splinter from scratching at the door."

Ken pursed his lips. His companion's theory was possible but it sounded weak, an effort to calm his nerves. "Maybe. I'd like to think so."

"Do you want to stay the night with me? You're most welcome. I know what you're thinking but I don't for one moment believe that hand has crawled up here. It's only interested in seeking revenge on those who mutilated it and their descendants, which lets you out."

"I guess so," Ken made an effort to believe the other. "I'll be okay. I'll keep the door locked and a wood chopper handy...just in case."

"It's up to you, Ken. And don't forget, we're going to fit another fishing trip in before you go home."

❖

Darkness had fallen and Ken had poured himself a stiff whisky. He knew only too well that sleep would be difficult tonight. Maybe he would forget the promised sea fishing trip with Bryn and leave for home tomorrow. Certainly he would never return here again.

Suddenly there came a loud knocking on the door that demanded an answer. He started, spilled some of his drink. God, who on earth could that be? Well, there was only one way to find out. His hand shook as he unlocked the door.

"Police," the taller of the two men outside displayed a card identifying himself as Detective Inspector Jones. His companion was obviously an assistant. "May we come inside and talk to you?"

"Sure," Ken held the door open, closed it after them. "How can I help you Inspector?" He indicated vacant chairs but his visitors ignored him.

"There's been a murder," the inspector's eyes were fixed unwaveringly on Ken, "down on the shore. A woman, as yet unidentified. My officers are currently making enquiries in the village. Possibly sometime last evening. She was discovered by a holidaymaker who spotted her body this afternoon after the tide receded. It would appear that she was killed before dark yesterday. A dog walker along the tideline informs us that he passed that way in the early evening and he would have seen her if she had been lying there. An autopsy will be carried out to confirm the cause of death. Her injuries are indicative of a violent killing."

Ken paled, began to shake visibly. "How terrible, have you any idea...?"

"Only that there's blood on your door handle, Mister Casey, and splashes of it on a stone slab nearby. Can you explain how the blood came to be there?"

"I...I noticed it when I returned from a fishing trip earlier."

"I see. One of my officers will be taking samples of the dried blood for DNA testing. Where were you, Mister Casey, between the hours of 7pm yesterday and 7am this morning?"

"I went sea fishing at 7am this morning with Mister Jones next door."

"And yesterday evening and during the night hours?"

"I...I was here. In this chalet."

"Is there anybody who can confirm that?"

"Mister Jones knows."

"But he was not with you?"

"No...I was all alone. You see, I had a nasty experience last year. I was shrimping and I caught a severed human hand. It was alive, crawled..."

"Oh, not that nonsense story again!" The officer's disbelief and impatience were evident in his retort. "Years ago, just after I joined the Force, there was a double murder down on that same beach. The locals spouted that same yarn about a mutilated hand. Absolute rubbish! Intense and lengthy police investigations failed to find the murderer. The case was eventually left on file but we can disregard all that poppycock. Now we have another murder and I intend to get to the bottom of it."

"I was only a kid in those days, inspector."

"Yes, I accept that you couldn't have been responsible for that double murder, but the fact is there's blood on your door handle and you don't appear to have cut your hand. I am pretty sure in my own mind that it came from the murdered woman. Furthermore, you have no witness to account for your movements during the night hours of yesterday and up until 7am today."

Ken Casey buried his face in his hands. Oh, Jesus, that gruesome hand that somehow lived after being severed from its arm had found another means of twisted revenge.

"I swear by Almighty God that I did not kill that woman on the beach!" A cry of despair.

"A DNA test from a blood sample on your door handle will prove or disprove that. I will organise that immediately and we should know the result by tomorrow. In the meantime you will be remanded in custody."

Head and shoulders bowed Ken Casey was led out to the police car. He knew only too well that the bloodstains on the door handle had come from the murdered woman down on the beach, left there by the crawling hand when it had come looking for him. There was no way he would be able to prove his innocence. A murder charge was a forgone conclusion.

Down on the beach, the hand had crawled into a heap of seaweed. It settled there to await the coming of another unsuspecting victim. Cledwyn's revenge for dismembering would be inflicted upon any who came his way, whether or not they were descendants of those who mutilated his body so long ago.

Serpent Bay

Johnny Mains

One day, towards the end of September, Brendan Court set out from Porth Stour, with the intention of walking about ten miles east along the Cornish coast. The morning had mostly been heavy and dull, cut with streams of soft moist warm air which came up strongly from the south-west. A prudent man would have accepted the warnings hung out in the sky and turned back, but Brendan kept on hoping against the signs of the weather. He was half-way into his journey when the heavens uttered a low, moaning sob, and a sharp gale from the south-west broke upon the coast, first bringing with it a heavy penetrating mist, and then driving, hissing sheets of rain, which made his face and hands smart, half-blinded him and wet him through to the skin.

When Brendan was thoroughly soaked he came to a crossroads, and recognising it from a previous walk many years before, knew that there was a quiet little inn hugging the edge of the beach. The landlord let him in, although the inn wasn't due to open until that evening. The landlord was a tall, stiff-looking man, however Brendan found him civil and obliging. He found him a set of flannels to dry himself with, and supplied a large, warm dressing-gown, and a pair of roomy slippers. He remarked with a throaty laugh that a glass of rum by the roaring fire in the bar was by far the best preventative measure against a certain chill. Once Brendan's clothes were drying by the fire, he sat down with his pipe; thankfully his tobacco was made out of sterner stuff than he and was as dry as a bone. The landlady, equally as stiff as her husband, set a steaming tumbler of rum by his elbow. Brendan lit his pipe, and began to feel grateful to the storm which had driven him into such a snug. His comfort was made complete when the landlord sat down opposite with his own tumbler of elixir. Placing it on the table between them, he lit the churchwarden held delicately between his thumb and finger.

"That's a sharp gale," Brendan said, taking a drink of the warmed rum and gasping with pleasure as it slowly made his insides glow.

"It'll be worse in a bit. You're going to be stuck here for a while, but I don't suppose you'd mind that," the landlord said with a smile, crossing his legs luxuriously and looking at the smoke which he blew from his lips into a shaggy cloud towards the high wide fireplace.

"Have you seen it this bad here before?" Brendan enquired, matching the landlord's plume of smoke with a dense fog of his own.

"Hell no!" he chuckled. "Why, there isn't water enough inshore for it. It's all sand and sand and sand below us, as far as the eye can see. At low water a man can walk out a mile. A very different coast from the one I used to live."

"Where was that?"

"Serpent Bay. Another fifteen miles round this coast. That's where you have a chance of getting a look at the sou'-wester and what it can do. All cliffs and rocks and huge boulders, and when the waves hit it, the spray is sent one hundred metres inland. It's quite a sight."

"I'm sure it must be" Brendan replied, taking a fresh mouthful of rum.

"Say, did you ever hear of the tragedy at Serpent Bay? A brig went down, the *Lanchester*, a hundred years ago."

"No, I'm only here on a walking holiday, I don't know the area at all. Perhaps you would be good enough to tell me?" Brendan said, perceiving the landlord had quite the story to tell, and certainly being in the mood to listen. The landlord smiled briefly, settled himself further into his easy chair, took a deep drink of wine from his glass, blew a few thoughtful puffs from his churchwarden and began.

"Serpent Bay faces sou'west. For miles the coast is harder than this stretch, like a cruel stepmother, it is. Serpent's Bay isn't more than half a mile wide at the opening but it expands inside; and a mile from the mouth it stops at a sandy strand. Now, once the Atlantic wallows into it on the back of a heavy, heavy sou'wester, no ship has a chance once she gets inside its jaws."

"Is Serpent's Bay a port?"

"No, it is not a port, so it's quite right that you ask what business a ship would have being there. All I can say is that accidents happen, and once every fifty years or so an unfortunate craft gets swept in. Once that happens it's as good as all over for her, and long odds against her crew. A rude slab of sea carried away the rudder of the *Lanchester* and that's how she came into the bay. Half-way in is a sandbank, and it's like the whole weight of the sea strikes it. In a gale there is always broken water on the bank, and when a vessel comes in, she grounds there and that is that. The *Lanchester* was flung on it broadside to the sea with a list to leeward. Waves dumped over her, and tons of water swept her decks. She was a large brig, and everyone watching the scene on shore soon saw to their horror that she had more passengers than crew. She had twenty-five sailors, eighty passengers, and there she lay, keeling over more with every wave that hit her, slowly being hammered to pieces on that sandbank. The sailors couldn't get the pinnaces free in time, and the first few waves swept them away from the ship, along with casks, water barrels, rigging..." The landlord took a pause and another drink of his wine.

"Surely there are lifeguards on such a dangerous bay?"

"Yes, there's a lifeboat helmed by local fisherman. Four times that lifeboat was launched, and four times she was tossed back like a child refusing vegetables at dinner. It's a hard thing for strong and willing men to fold their arms while people are perishing before their eyes. About twenty minutes later there was a sound like a bomb going off. That's when the ship cleft in two – the main mast fell over and the foremast began swaying, one this way and the other that, like two drunk men trying to pass each other in a bar." The landlord chuckled dryly at his analogy. "All on the shore knew what was going to happen now. The broken water, which had been white and boiling, grew black and heavy with human forms, and as dusk started to fall, cargo and bodies began to come ashore. By night the wind had fallen to nothing more than a light breeze. Sixteen living and fifty-seven dead. The living were taken up to Effingham, a town about four miles from the Bay, and the dead – men, women and children alike – were laid out in one long, ghastly line on the beach above high water. At each end of the line a fire was lighted. One coastguard was set to tend the fire and watch the dead, while every other person old enough and strong enough was engaged in saving and securing the cargo. The coastguard who watched by the dead never forgot that night. As the clothes of the victims dried they began to stir in the breeze. Scores of times he thought he saw a leg, or an arm, or a head raised. Scores of times he thought he heard a cry. By midnight the coastguard was half dead with terror and he thought that if he was to have one more scare, his heart might burst. As the moon began to blink through a torn sky, the coastguard felt that he must have some kind of company or go mad. It was near low water, and the people working at the salvage were a good way off. He was at the fire furthest from the workers. He stooped and picked up a few pieces of wood, and tended the fire so that it might be all right while he was gone to fetch company. Before rising from his crouching posture, he glanced over his shoulder down the long, ghastly line of the dead, and he noticed a change had taken place in that line. He turned his head further round and saw standing over him a figure – the figure of a woman – the figure of one of the dead! With a yell, he rose and jumped back. "'I am so cold," said the figure.

"Oh, I am as cold as death. I need to be warmed up." The woman threw herself onto the man and they tussled for a while before the coastguard managed to break free, screaming to the crowd down by the water. As soon as he could speak he told what had happened. A dozen men ran back with him. They found a woman, dazed and shivering, kneeling on the ground with her face turned towards the fire. When she looked at the men, her face was smeared with blood. With all their attention on her, nobody noticed that the coastguard had been bitten by the woman. Quite severely, in fact, and he was starting to lose all sensations, both physical and mental. The coastguard staggered off into the dunes, unable to believe that he was dying, his clothes utterly soaked in blood. He was never found, his body was assumed lost during the rescue. How was anyone to know that the wreck had been engineered by the woman herself? It's very dangerous for a vampire to be immersed in saltwater, but she knew that if she didn't do something, the person who had been following her for weeks, the person who had joined the ship as it left the port of Gdark, Romania, that person would try to kill her..."

Brendan guffawed. "Ha! You almost had me! Droll, very droll. A nice vampire tale to get me through the night."

"You don't believe?" asked the landlord. "Permit me to introduce myself to you as that coastguard, and let me also introduce you to the woman who that night stood up over me by the fire, the woman who found me in the dunes and finished off the ceremony, giving me her blood to drink. The woman who later became my wife,"

Brendan looked on, confusion and creeping terror stalking his features. The landlady sat knitting at the bar and smiled benignly. "I don't recollect anything," she said, "from the time I was washed off the vessel until all the people were round me. I don't remember biting Tom by the fire, and it was by chance that I found his body and realised what it was I had done, and the opportunity I had given myself. England was a new place to me, and I would need a companion."

"Well," said the landlord, knocking the ashes out of his pipe, "you can see Tom by the fire now, my dear, and Tom's glass is empty."

"Of course my love." The landlady got up from behind the bar and walked towards her husband, taking his empty glass from him. Brendan was frozen, unable to move as he realised that he was in a public house of untold evil...

The landlady's hand moved swiftly across Brendan's throat, and she held her glass under the slice she had created. The glass filled up rather quickly. The landlady licked the blood from her wickedly sharp nails, passing the glass to her husband as Brendan's limp body fell to the floor.

"Take him out later, love. The fishes will like the taste of him, he looks after himself."

Tom looked at his wife lovingly.

"Yes dear."

Chimera
Rosalie Parker

Chimera – A fire-breathing female monster with a lion's head, a hair-covered body, and a serpent's tail, or, a thing which is hoped for but is illusory or impossible to achieve.

The incoming tide nudged gently at the line of seaweed and broken shells. Her eyes were on the horizon, her bare toes dug into the sand.

It was entrancing, the first light soft and pure. Julie scanned the far waters, hand shielding her eyes, but the sea's green glassy surface mocked her, a carapace over the murky depths beneath. She took some photographs, but they could not capture the beauty of the day. Once more she had a presentiment that the thing so desired would not show itself and, after a while, she headed back to the hostel. Despite a flicker of disappointment, hope resurfaced. She had been unlucky today, but there was always tomorrow, or the day after that...

The room was small, a single bed the dominant feature. In one corner stood a rust-stained enamel sink. Julie took her camera from her bag and scrolled again through the photos she had taken. She hung her jacket in the flimsy wardrobe and continued with her daily routine – breakfast, then down the hall to the shower. There was a queue.

"It's only just been fixed."

Above the spray of the shower they could hear singing.

"His benefits came through," said Christine. "Lucky him. I went to the food bank yesterday. You'd be amazed at the kind of people who were there."

After her shower Julie walked through the awakening town to the library. She looked for jobs on the computer, then searched the shelves for something to read. As she reached for a book, another flashback hit her: She was on the landing, screaming as the fire burnt through the door. The fireman shouted at her to get back and smashed the door down with his axe. Inside was an inferno, the heat indescribable.

Julie sat down and took deep breaths. Three months before, a fire had destroyed her flat and possessions, including her books and laptop. Stored on the computer were four years' worth of films and photographs. The flat was rented and she had no insurance, and it was her good fortune that she had been out with her camera when the blaze first took hold. It was thought that a petrol-soaked rag had been lit and stuffed through her letter box, although no traces of accelerant were found. She couldn't bear to think about who would have done such a thing. The horror and uncertainty of it gnawed at her.

Julie knew she should be grateful that the council had found her a room in the hostel. Her estranged father, away on an extended visit to her brother in Australia, had so far failed to stump up the loan that would help get her back on her feet. Her only hope was to take and sell more photographs. She had built a reputation for unusual subjects beautifully shot; there were plenty of picture editors happy to consider her work. But to be able to afford her own place she needed something special - a picture or piece of film associated with a great story. Then her agent could orchestrate a bidding war and her troubles, for a while at least, would be over.

She had some modest successes. On a twilight walk along the cliff path she took a photo of lightening striking a hawthorn tree. It appeared on the front page of the *Daily Telegraph*. There was always a market for pictures of extreme weather, and animals. But, despite living cheaply, Julie had been unable to save enough money for a deposit on a flat. The hostel was shabby and noisy and she had to keep her door locked because of the drug taking and pilfering that went on.

The Red Lion was as good a pub as any in which to drown her sorrows. Nestling in the Old Town it had oak panelled walls and an open fire, and was frequented by real ale enthusiasts and tourists, as well as locals. As Julie nursed her beer she listened in to a conversation between two men at an adjacent table. They were fishermen: she recognised one as Michael Duggan.

"...It rose up in front of me, then dived back under, too quick for me to make out much,' he was saying. 'It was big, though; the head was massive, like nothing I've seen before. I asked my father about it. He said to talk to one of the old timers. According to Jimmy Laidlaw there've been a few sightings over the years. Never very far out. They keep it quiet. It's supposed to be bad luck if you see it."

"You're pulling my leg," said his friend.

"Believe what you like. I'm a pretty sceptical person, but I know I saw something. The next day one of the flats went up in smoke."

Julie was intrigued, and the reference to the fire which destroyed her home was troubling. Researching in the library she found a paragraph in the *Victoria County History* that described the local myth of a 'great fire-breathing beast' living in the seas around the bay. The earliest recorded sightings dated to the seventeenth century. It was said to have been seen before the devastating storm of 1854, and was supposed to have the head of a lion, a hair-covered female body and a snake's tail. *Pretty comical* she thought, although perhaps there was some garbled truth in the myth; the creature could be a whale or a basking shark seen from an unusual angle. That would still be of interest. She sniffed the beginnings of a story.

So Julie began her daily trips to the beach. If she could photograph the creature, whatever it was, or better still film it, the story might go global. Part of her knew it was a sign of her desperation that she gave credence to Michael's tale, but the potential rewards made her visits worthwhile. It wasn't as if she had anything better to do.

Only Christine knew about Julie's pilgrimages to the shore.

"You're wasting your time. It's a fisherman's yarn: he was winding up his mate. You'd be better off doing something useful."

"Taking photos is the only thing I want to do. Anyway, I've been applying for jobs for weeks. No one wants to know. If I can take one amazing photo or shoot an earth-shattering film I'll be set up for life."

Every morning Julie kept the faith. On stormy days tall clouds massed to the west. Pummelled by the wind, she struggled along the shore, her cheap coat failing to keep out the rain.

One day, in despair, she flung out her arms and yelled "Where are you? Show yourself."

A stray gust of wind snatched her words away.

It was easy to track down Michael Duggan. A few enquiries sent her back to the Red Lion, where Julie approached him and asked if they could talk. The pub was busy; there were no tables free so they stood at the bar. He accepted her offer of a pint.

"I'd like to pick your brains," Julie said. She explained that she had heard his conversation in the pub several weeks before.

"What do you want to know?"

"Tell me what happened."

He repeated the story, without embellishment.

"I don't expect to be believed," he said.

The latticework of lines around his eyes came into sharper focus as he leaned towards her. His face was weather-beaten and although he looked weary, his eyes flicked over her.

"Why the interest?"

"I'm a photographer. If there's a new species out there, I'd like to get it on camera."

Michael laughed. "It would make your fortune."

"I'd cut you in if you'll take me out in your boat."

He leant back. "Really? You believe me then?"

"We could prove the doubters wrong."

He considered, then shrugged.

"I could use the money. What do I have to lose?"

They had chosen a still afternoon and the waters beyond the bay were relatively calm, the usual swell soothed by the tranquil weather. Julie took out her camera and cleaned the lens carefully, then rechecked the battery, even though she knew she had charged it earlier in the day.

"Ready?" Michael called from the wheelhouse.

Julie, standing at the bow, waved her assent. She felt adrenaline surge through her. Switching the camera to video mode, and focusing on the middle distance, she panned around the boat, her finger ready on the zoom.

Ahead, a flock of gannets had gathered, diving and resurfacing with fish in their beaks. Other seabirds circled overhead. Michael reined in the throttle and the boat slowed to a crawl. He joined Julie at the bow.

"There's a shoal of pilchards down there. It's not just the birds that take them. You sometimes see dolphins, sharks, even whales."

"And the occasional unidentified sea creature?"

"Well it has to eat something."

"Do you think we'll see it today?"

Michael laughed. "You'll have to be patient. I would've thought that's a necessity in your job."

The gannets dived again and again, folding their wings against their bodies as they pierced the water.

Michael returned to the wheelhouse and cut the engine.

"Why did you call your boat *Monster*?" Julie asked.

"It's a bit of a beast. I named it a long time before I saw the creature."

The gannets rose from the water and flew eastwards.

"The shoal's moved on," Michael said.

Monster followed the coast, Julie's eyes on her camera screen. Apart from the seabirds, there was no sign of life. After several hours' fruitless searching, they called it a day.

As they entered the harbour, Michael said, "We'll go out again at the weekend."

That night Julie dreamt she and Michael were scuba diving: they were at some depth, just above the sea bed. She was filming with a waterproof camera. Michael, swimming beside her, steered them towards a shoal of curious-looking fish. As they swam closer she could see they had lions' heads, hair-covered bodies and snakes' coiling tails. The strange little fish began rooting in the sea bed, stirring up detritus so that it was impossible to see more than a few metres ahead. Michael grabbed her arm. There was a surge in the water and a huge shape swam past. It was impossible to see the thing clearly. When she looked down she saw that she had gripped the camera so hard it had broken in two...

She woke, got out of bed and checked her own camera. It was in one piece. The dream stayed with her and it was nearly dawn before she went back to sleep.

The worst of the storm had yet to hit, but the sea was already raging and waves thundered onto the beach. Julie took photographs of the surf and the dark distant clouds.

Everything was lit by a numinous glow; the air brimmed with expectation. Suddenly the light changed. She looked through the photos: they were disappointing, grey and indistinct, lacking the energy of the day.

Julie was hungry; she had been on the beach since dawn. Christine would be waiting for her in the Old Town. One last time Julie looked out to sea, then slipped the camera into her rucksack.

Christine was waiting outside the Town Hall. They headed for the market and ate lunch sitting on the War Memorial steps. After a few moments Christine said:

"They're threatening to throw me out of the hostel."

"Why?"

"Apparently, I've had my room long enough and I should be trying to get my own place. I told them that's not going to be easy, but there's a long waiting list and they have to think of others. I don't know what I'm going to do."

"Surely they'll help you find somewhere?"

"You know how few vacant flats there are. And they're expensive dumps."

"I expect I'll be next," said Julie. "I've been there nearly as long as you."

"We could get a place together."

Julie smiled. "I'd like that."

It would take a miracle for them to find the money.

Time, she realised, was against her.

Julie had not sold a picture for weeks, and her agent was becoming impatient. Even the thought of tomorrow's boat trip with Michael could not distract her from self-pity. Last weekend they had gone out on rough seas. She discovered that she was a bad sailor, and had been relieved when they turned for home. Apart from her seasickness the trip was uneventful. Even the many porpoises that visited the bay eluded them.

Calls to her father were unanswered. Funds were running low, and she could not claim benefits until her money was as good as gone. Christine was about to move out of the hostel into a run-down bed and breakfast on the sea front. As Julie had predicted, the hostel manager had approached her and asked if she too would start looking for somewhere else to live.

She took her camera out of her bag and studied the film she had taken during the rough trip out. Grey water churned, seagulls squawked. There was not a spark of interest in it, except for some incidental shots of Michael in the wheelhouse, looking out to sea.

The storms had given way to a sullen, overcast day. *Monster* skimmed over the calm waters of the bay. As they reached the open sea Michael opened the throttle a little and they cruised in wide circles. Julie attached her camera to the tripod, but her heart wasn't in it. Sensing her depression, Michael put his hand on her shoulder.

"We'll find the bloody thing," he'd said. "It can't hide forever."

"I'm in trouble, Michael."

"Something will turn up"

Porpoises raced each other in *Monster's* wake. Gannets dived in the distance.

"There's a shoal," Michael shouted, and steered the boat towards the birds. Julie prepared the camera for close-ups. As they neared the feeding area she spotted something floating in the water.

"Cut the engine!" she yelled at Michael. She leaned over the side.

A grey shape bobbed on the waves.

"It's a porpoise. Or it was."

Blood darkened the water.

"Just the tail-end, poor thing."

Michael surveyed the remains.

"Look at the way it's been savaged."

Julie turned to him. "Are we on to something?"

"I don't know."

He went back to the wheelhouse and the boat picked up speed. As they neared the birds Michael cut the engine and Julie took shot after shot of the gannets diving. When she reviewed the pictures they seemed hackneyed, but Michael praised them.

"I can tell you're a professional," he said.

She thought, *He's just being kind.*

Just then *Monster* began to yaw.

"Hold tight!" Michael shouted.

Julie grasped the rail. Something swam underneath and brushed against the keel: the boat shuddered. The gannets rose from the water and flew silently away.

Julie cried out, more in triumph than fear.

The Red Lion was almost empty and they chose a table near the fire. Julie watched Michael as he bought drinks at the bar.

"We were so close to seeing it..." she said when he returned.

He sighed. "It could've been a humpback."

Julie reached for his hand.

"We're going to see it, aren't we?"

He gently removed her fingers.

"There are no guarantees. Look, Julie..."

"Are you bored with it?"

"I should never have raised your hopes. "

"We were close," she said fiercely. "I want it so much, Michael."

The party began in the late afternoon and continued for most of the night. Julie gave up trying to sleep and read her library book in bed. From time to time the night manager asked for quiet and the decibels lessened, only to rise again when he retreated to his office.

Julie watched from her window as night shaded into morning, then dressed and let herself out of the building. She saw no one. The brief walk was equally free of human activity, although the seagulls called out from their cliff-face perches. As she stepped onto the beach she stopped to take off her shoes. Cool sand trickled between her toes.

The rising sun gave light to a calm, clear day. She pulled the camera from her rucksack and walked to the gently foaming surf, where a cluster of empty shells rolled in its ebb and flow. She took photographs and some film. The thought came to her that she would rather die than move away from the sea.

Her father rang, only to announce that he was staying in Australia for as long as his visa allowed. He said, when she asked him for a loan, that she was old enough to fend for herself; it would do her good, and she should find a cheaper town in which to live. Julie could not bring herself to beg for money. When she explained about the dire straits she was in, he said, 'You'd better find yourself a boyfriend.'

The shock of it rearranged her thoughts. She felt that for the first time in months she was thinking clearly. The myth of the monster was just that – a legend to spice up an evening tale, a story passed down through the generations. The power of suggestion had bewitched Michael and the old fishermen, conjuring false sightings. She had stupidly allowed herself to believe that it might be true.

I've been a fool, she thought.

Julie sold some photographs. Christine found a job waitressing and managed to slip her a few free meals. Julie saved a little money.

Michael offered to take her out again in *Monster*. She aimed to spend the trip taking a series of photographs of the coast from the sea. Her agent had pitched the idea to a Sunday supplement and they had expressed an interest in publishing the pictures.

Michael looked exhausted. When she commented on this he said "Fishing's a tough way to make a living."

"I thought you enjoyed it."

"I used to," he said.

"What's changed?"

He shrugged. "Fish stocks are falling. I'm getting older, I suppose..."

Julie watched him, surreptitiously filmed him, took a photo or two.

They spotted a school of porpoises, leaping over each

other in their haste to reach the open sea. The seagulls were flying back to land.

"Is there bad weather on the way?" she asked.

"The forecast's good."

She took some pictures of the cliffs.

Michael said quietly "You've stopped believing, haven't you."

"No... It's just that..."

"I've been thinking that we might as well give up."

"I enjoy these trips," she found herself saying. "I enjoy being with you."

"Julie..."

She put her hands over her ears.

The sea lapped against the hull. Michael opened the throttle and turned the boat for home.

As they entered the bay *Monster* began to rock violently. All around them, the water churned.

"Grab the rail!" Michael cried, cutting the engine. It was too late. Julie tumbled over the side and into the sea. As she surfaced the cold made her gasp and she inhaled more water. She swam aimlessly around, remembering at last to inflate her life jacket. Michael threw in a life ring with a rope attached, but she couldn't reach it. *Monster* was drifting away.

"I'll get help," he called out, and picked up the radio handset.

The air was still, the sky cloudless, but the sea threw her around like a doll. Panic seized her as she felt her strength drain away. She had swallowed a great deal of water.

Michael shouted, "I've called the coastguard. The lifeboat'll be here in a few minutes."

Julie turned over and floated on her back. The cold ate into her bones. She knew she would not have long before hypothermia set in. Michael started *Monster's* engine and the boat inched towards her.

"Hold on," he said. "Stay awake!"

The sea boiled and out of it rose the creature. It writhed, exposing its hair-covered torso and, thrashing its scaly tail, shot tall plumes of water into the air. Fire flared from its nostrils, illuminating the snarling leonine face. It dwarfed the crazily rocking boat. The beast reared up and opened its jaws, revealing scythe-like fangs. As its eyes locked onto Julie's, she slipped into unconsciousness...

Michael sat by the bed while Julie slept. They had warmed her carefully and a touch of pink suffused her cheeks. She woke slowly, stretching her body before opening her eyes.

"Michael," she said, and smiled.

"I didn't think you'd make it," he said.

"Well, here I am."

A while later, she asked sleepily "Did you take some photos?"

"I was too busy helping to pull you out of the water."

"Not of me, of the creature!"

"What are you talking about?"

"It was there!"

Michael shook his head. "I'll come clean. I'm sorry. I bet my friend I could persuade you the thing was real. It got out of hand."

"But I saw it!"

"Hypothermia does funny things to people."

"You're saying it's all in my head."

She thought for a moment.

"I don't believe you. Where's my camera?"

"It went over the side with you."

Julie, exhausted, closed her eyes and drifted away.

It was best to make sure. Lifting her head he slowly pulled out the pillow. She did not wake, and he laid it gently on her face. The nurse had shut the door on her way out and it should be some time before she returned. He took hold of the pillow and pressed down hard. Julie barely stirred.

When it was over he replaced the pillow beneath her head. She was beautifully still, an angel in her white hospital gown. He sat down and waited for the nurse.

After he had answered their questions, they sent him home.

He reviewed the pictures. They were astonishing, incontrovertible.

It was time to find himself an agent.

The Perfect Day to Be at Sea
Kayleigh Marie Edwards

Eric Cousins hoped that people were still searching for him, but what he hoped and what he knew were different things. That they would have given up and assumed him dead long ago was just about the only thing that he did know for certain. A lot of what he thought he knew had changed. There had been a time when he had known that the darkest, coldest thing was the night. Now he knew that there was something worse; the sea was far darker and colder. At least the night yielded eventually to the day. The sea, however, was unrelenting, and even under the highest sun, it remained like ice. And worst – worst of all – the sea contained nightmares unimaginable to even the most vivid of dreamers. The sea was full of terror.

Eric treaded water, kicking his legs in wide arcs. He didn't know how long he had been bobbing in the waves alone. He didn't remember how he had come to be in the water in the first place. All he remembered was that he had initially come out on a boat. But it was gone now. All that there was, all that he could see for miles and miles in every direction, was sea. No boat, no land, no sign of anything anywhere. His eyes burned with salt and he could barely make out where the horizon began. The water was thick and murky and dark and he could hardly see his own legs, never mind what lurked beneath them. He was too preoccupied to notice that the water was much dirtier and darker than usual. There was nothing that stood out, yet it all looked familiar somehow. Perhaps, he thought, it was just because everything looked the same.

His chest was tight and his breathing was ragged. How could this be? Where was his boat? Had he fallen overboard? But if so, why had his crewmates not fished him out? Had they left him to die or had the ship gone down somehow? All were questions that bothered him, like a fly buzzing in the back of his mind, but his most prominent, consuming thought, was that he did not want to die.

His lungs filling with water, the unbearable pressure in his chest.

Had that been a dream? He wasn't sure, but he was still alive so he guessed so.

Eric was a man who was not used to his desires conflicting with reality. Generally speaking, when he wanted something, he got it - a job, a woman, a particular physique, a goal to obtain, it didn't matter what it was. Nothing had ever been out of Eric's reach; he had never even had to consider the possibility of failure. He was a winner. Now he was at the mercy of something much bigger and stronger than he was, and his confidence had slipped away beneath the waves.

He called for help and flinched at the cracked sound of his voice, which was tiny and weak. His cries seemed to go nowhere before sinking into the depths. It was like the sea itself had simply reached up and pulled it under, just like it was trying to do to him.

For a while, he continued to tread water, only moving as and where the waves pushed him. He didn't know what to do. He squinted up at the sun, which seemed to be setting rapidly. It occurred to him that it would be dark soon, and the thought of floating in the vast expanse of ocean in the pitch black chilled him to his core.

Think! Eric commanded himself, trying to muster the courage that he was devoid of. He turned in all directions, staring as far as his eyes would allow, hoping for a glimpse of anything to head towards. But there was nothing. Anxiety nestled deep within his abdomen, twisting his tummy and hurting him.

He wished he knew more about the sea. He wished he'd paid more attention to his father on his sailing lessons. He came from a long line of sea-faring men. His father had been a fisherman, his grandfather a sailor, and his great-grandfather a sea captain. As far back as Eric knew, every first-born man in his family had shared a passion for the water, as well as a first name. Unfortunately, that was where his common traits with his predecessors ended, because unlike those who came before him, Eric was a lazy student. He could drive small boats, and was an average sailor, but all those lessons his father had tried to impress upon him about the ways of the sea had fallen on deaf ears. It was too much like hard work to learn all of the minute details that seemed so important now.

A wave engulfed him, only for a moment, but that was

enough to drive Eric's quiet fear into complete panic. He broke the surface after only a second, gasping and spitting out salt, and crying. He turned around in a circle, once again searching in vain in all directions once again for any sign of humanity. What was it his father had told him about the tide? Did the waves move towards or away from the coast?

He tried to focus, tried to remember some long-lost lesson from years ago that could help him now. Away. He decided that the waves moved *away* from the coast, which meant that while he'd been treading water, he had just allowed himself to drift further out to sea.

He started swimming against the tide, suddenly invigorated. Earlier, he and his friends had taken his father's yacht but they hadn't come too far out. They never did. Though he had told his friends differently, Eric knew that he wasn't equipped to deal with much, should an emergency arise. He had never sailed, *could* never sail, too far out from the coast because he wasn't even sure how to handle a storm. They had just come out a little way, not even far enough to lose sight of the coast, dropped anchor, and drank some beers under the sun. From there, his memory failed him. However, he assumed that somehow he had gone overboard, and that his friends had gone back to shore for help. It troubled him that he had no memory of such an event, or even of swimming back up to the surface in time to see his no-good 'friends' just take off with his yacht, but he supposed that perhaps he'd hit his head.

He couldn't have been in the water long otherwise he would have drowned, so he figured that though the tide had most definitely carried him further than they'd sailed, it couldn't have carried him *too* much further. Eric was practically grinning with this realisation. Swimming against the tide was actually much more difficult than he expected, especially for someone as strong and fit as he was, but any minute now, his efforts would be rewarded when the land came into view. Perhaps the coastguard would find him first, but either way, twenty minutes from now, he'd be on dry land.

He was cold and his arms and legs started to ache, which annoyed him because he'd barely been swimming for five minutes. He made a mental note to spend more time in the gym, and then started to work on the ways in which he was going to punish his friends for leaving him behind. *I could have drowned*, he thought.

But I didn't, and any minute now... Eric risked a glance up. Still no shore. He dipped his head back down and focused on swimming. His limbs and core burned, and saltwater splashed into his mouth and eyes, but he got used to the taste and the discomfort and did his best to ignore it. All that mattered was moving forward.

He continued to swim.

Any minute now.

The temperature dropped.

Any minute now.

The sunlight waned.

Any. Minute. Now.

It went dark.

He stopped swimming, frozen with the cold and with an alien but undeniable terror. He started treading water again, wondering how he could have failed to notice the light disappearing as the sun went down. A violent wave pushed him forward and he choked as water went down his throat. He realised that he was now going with the waves instead of against them, and had a mind-shattering moment of confusion in which he just couldn't fathom how he could have possibly turned around despite swimming forwards the whole time. Then, it occurred to him that swimming against the waves in the first place was probably the wrong move. He thought back to lying on the beach and watching the waves lap the shore, and felt so stupid. Of course waves headed *towards* the coast. Or did they? Did they even move in one direction at all? It dawned on him that he knew a lot less than he had always given himself credit for.

Eric treaded water, motionless from the waist up. He was so cold and it was so dark, but dark was an understatement. There was no moon and he could see no stars. He could see nothing. The turn of night had rendered him blind. His throat was already raw from unintentionally gulping down dirty saltwater, but he screamed for help anyway. Eventually, he stopped screaming for help, and just screamed.

The complete darkness was disorientating. Eric would have moments where he'd wait for his eyes to adjust, only to realise that they wouldn't, because there wasn't so much as a sliver of light for them to adjust to. It was like being in a vacuum.

He'd been abroad to tropical places and enjoyed seasides where the water was so clear that you could see all the way down to the seabed. Off the coast of Cornwall, however, he couldn't expect such luxury. UK waters were polluted and murky, and even when the sun had been up, he hadn't been able to see a thing below him. Only now though, did that strike him as odd. He'd been swimming in this sea plenty of times and never noticed a complete lack of underwater vision before. It hadn't been much of a concern a few hours ago, because the other thing that UK seas lacked were dangerous, tropical sea creatures. It had never once occurred to him that he could be attacked by something like a shark, because that wasn't usually a real problem in British waters. But now that it was pitch black, and he couldn't even see his own hands or the water he was in, he wondered.

There weren't any dangerous sharks, but hadn't his father said something about whales?

Goddamnit, why hadn't he listened?

Did whales attack people? He didn't know.

Eric treaded water, completely blind. He tried to hold in his tears at first, feeling ashamed and weak, but after a while he could restrain it no longer. Every time a thought occurred to him, it made his situation worse. It was so dark and it would be for hours and hours. He was already so cold, going numb all over, and it would continue to get colder. He was more tired than he'd ever been, than he ever even thought could be possible. He wondered if what he felt was true exhaustion. His body screamed at him to rest, but he continued. He thought that if he stopped kicking for even a moment, he would slip under the surface and that would be the end. Keeping himself afloat was now more than a challenge, but he had no doubt that if he let himself become submerged, kicking his way back up would be harder.

And in this darkness, would he even know which way was up at all?

A worse thought occurred to him. He'd managed to swim and keep his head above the water for a long time, and for all that time, he'd been convinced that it was just temporary. It was just a matter of keeping himself afloat until rescue arrived or he made it back to shore himself. He'd been swimming for a long time and had seen no sign of land, and now he worried that he'd made the grave error of swimming even further out. Direction was now completely lost to him, he had no bearings whatsoever.

Then the worst thought of all hit him. If he were likely to be rescued, it would have happened by now. If his friends had made it back and alerted the coastguard, surely he would have been picked up? Why had no one come for him?

As he bobbed there in the dark, he realised the horrible truth that if they hadn't found him in the day, they wouldn't be out looking for him in the dark. By now, he'd be assumed dead. The only thing anyone on land would be doing was waiting for his body to wash up somewhere.

Eric treaded water, more afraid than he could have ever believed possible. He was lost and helpless, his chest and throat on fire, and he was completely alone.

Her hair was the colour of fire and Eric had never seen a face so beautiful. On first glance, she had a smile that could light up a room. But when he looked deeper, there was something horrible under it. It was a good thing he and his friends had come along. What was she doing swimming alone so far out?

Eric's eyes opened wide. He was drowning. Disorientated and frantic, he forced himself to keep his eyes open despite the discomfort and lack of vision, and kicked. He swam in the direction that felt like 'up' for much longer than expected, before breaking the surface and emerging from one darkness into another with a sound that was half a gasp for air and half a sob.

He took a moment to clear his throat and nose, which stung, and he cried. The last thing he remembered was being wide awake and willing his freezing limbs to keep him afloat, and then the next thing he knew, he was waking up because his lungs were filling with water. He couldn't even remember feeling tired. Had he passed out? It didn't seem likely, yet it did feel oddly familiar.

Eric had had the feeling the entire time that something, besides the obvious, was very wrong. He'd woken up twice under water now, but with no recollection of how he slipped under in the first place. Then, of course, there were the gaps in his memory. The complete blank about how he'd come to be in the water in the first place bothered him the most, as did the question of how his yacht could have disappeared, apparently immediately after he fell overboard. It just didn't add up.

His dream started to come back to him in pieces. *He and his friends on the yacht. Drinks. Laughter. He finished a beer and leaned over the railing to throw the bottle as far as possible into the sea. A blur of flaming red underneath the water, and then she emerged, smiling up at him.*

Eric treaded water, praying for the sun to come up, but he knew it would be hours yet. He prayed that he could just survive until the morning, and he hoped more than ever that a rescue team would pick him up. Pray, pray, pray. Hope, hope, hope.

He was surprised that he'd managed to survive this long, that his body was complying with his will to live. He was actually impressed by himself, but that was nothing new. What was new was the silence; he couldn't stand it. There was only the sound of the waves, and it was starting to drive him crazy. It was like the sea was mocking him. He started to hum an indistinct song that he had a vague memory of hearing but couldn't remember where or who from. He knew he was alone, but the sound of a human voice, even just his own, was soothing.

Something big smashed into his hip. Eric screamed and looked around, although that was pointless because he was still blinded by the night. He whimpered, turning from side to side. He wanted to just freeze solid until whatever it was went away, but he couldn't because he needed to keep his legs and arms moving. The fear that he might touch something under the water was so severe that he didn't even notice that he was screaming inaudible words into the darkness. A minute passed where nothing happened, and he started to calm down. He took a few deep breaths, pressing his hand to his hip to make sure he wasn't injured.

"Okay, it's okay, it's okay," he whispered. He closed his eyes and it made him feel a bit better. It made no difference to his vision but choosing to shut everything out gave him a sense of control. He tried not to imagine what it could have been, because everything his mind conjured up was some distorted version of something that wanted to eat him. He'd only been afraid of drowning at first; now he realised there were worse ways to die out here.

He started to hum the old song again and considered swimming. But where? He supposed that any direction was useless anyway, and it wasn't like he could see where he was going. He decided to just stay still and try not to let his cramping muscles get the best of him. He didn't want to risk passing land by because he couldn't see it, and swimming without sight was too horrifying to endure. Just floating was already disorientating and agonising enough. Another uncomfortable sense of déjà vu swept over him.

His eyes were as sore and as tired as the rest of him, but he didn't dare close them. It would only take a second to nod off and slip into the depths again, and next time he might not make it back up.

His lungs filling with water, the unbearable pressure in his chest.

His humming took on a weird tone as he tensed up. The question of what to do was now incessant. Even though he'd decided to do nothing - there was nothing that could be done, after all - the idea that he *ought* to do something kept nagging at him.

Something broke the surface and splashed behind him. His voice quivered but he continued to hum. *It's just a whale, a friendly whale* he told himself. *Just a curious sea creature being nosey. Just don't panic, don't make yourself look like food.* The idea of being food to some unseen abomination made him feel sick. He vowed that if he survived this ordeal then he would never eat meat again, and commended himself for his newfound vegetarianism. Then he broke his own tune with a startled laugh at how ridiculous his thought process was.

There was another splash, but it came from a different direction further away. He sighed with relief; whatever it was had grown bored and was going away. He carried on humming, wondering where on earth he had heard the song, feeling more comforted than ever. If he could just keep himself company until daylight, it would be okay. Everything was less scary in the day. But he was so cold now.

The 'something' bumped into his legs and he screamed again. He could hear more splashes around him now, three or four in quick succession. So quick, in fact, that the speed of whatever it was made him think of sharks again. He realised with deeply accelerating horror that the thing hadn't been going away after all, and that it seemed to be toying with him. He licked his cracked lips and, for a moment, his body faltered and his head almost dipped under the water. He kicked harder than ever and then forced his legs to slow down.

More splashes. More bumps under the water. When it occurred to him that it was circling him, he would have screamed yet again had he not been too terrified to utter a sound.

There are no sharks, he reminded himself. He searched his memories for the things his father had told him, for any information that would comfort him now. He was sure there were no sharks, but what else would circle him? He panicked, remembering something his father had said about basking sharks. There were *those* sharks in the UK but were they dangerous to humans? He didn't think so, but he couldn't recall. He had never heard about any shark attacks so perhaps not, but if they didn't attack people then why wasn't it going away? He suddenly laughed when he realised he was sweating because it seemed absurd to him that he could sweat while most of him was under water.

His laughter sounded alien to him at first. Sound took on weird qualities when it didn't echo back whatsoever. He'd never noticed that before because, he supposed, he'd never before been in a vast open space laughing like a lunatic.

It took him a few minutes to realise that the alien sound wasn't his own laughter, but another sound. It was the same song that he'd been humming to himself; only it wasn't him singing it.

He almost dipped under the surface again as he froze in confusion and yet another wave of terror washed over him. It was most definitely a female voice, or perhaps *voices* since the song seemed to be coming from all around. He despaired over the idea that he had lost his mind so quickly. He'd been in the water for a matter of hours and had already gone mad, which disappointed him because he'd always thought of himself as the strong and sturdy type, inside and out. The song wasn't being hummed, but sung, with growing volume. There were no words, just a series of 'ahhhs' that were simultaneously beautiful and melodic, and otherworldly and horrifying.

Eric burst into laughter again and this time, he couldn't compose himself. He was going to die out here, alone at sea, with no real knowledge of how he had come to be in this situation in the first place. He was freezing, almost out of strength, and almost out of the will to keep himself afloat, and now he had gone insane too. It was as though his own mind was serenading his inescapable demise.

He laughed harder and louder, trying to drown out the singing. The angelic voice was beginning to take on a sinister, off-key tone. It took all of his energy to try to drown it out with his own manic, rasping laughter and just when he was succeeding, the singing voice filled his head. That was when he accepted that although it was impossible, her voice wasn't just a figment of his imagination. She was real and now she was forcing her song into his head as well as into his ears. He flinched and closed his eyes, shaking his head to try and shake out the song, but it was no use. Her voice bounced around behind his eyes, and the disorientation somehow dislodged more fragments of his dream.

Red hair that looked like fire, framing a flawless female face. He looked over the side of the boat and saw her swimming alone down there. The murky water somehow sparkled around her in the sunlight. She smiled up at him with brilliant white teeth.

"What are you doing swimming this far out, love?" he asked her. "The water is dangerous out here."

"I'm a strong swimmer," she replied, and then laughed as though she'd made a joke. He didn't get it, but he laughed anyway. She was the most beautiful woman he'd ever seen, and what were the odds that he should meet her out here like this. He didn't believe in such things, but all the same he wondered if this was fate.

Eric turned to his friends and told them to pass him the life ring he kept on board, which they did. He checked that the attached rope was securely tied to it and then threw it out. It landed in the water next to her but she only looked at it.

"Come aboard!" he smiled. She stared at him for a moment, distrustful. Her eyes went to his friends and then back to him. "Come on, sweetheart," he laughed, motioning for her to grab the life ring. She started to smile again, but this time there was something threatening in it somehow.

"Why don't you come down here instead?" she asked. Eric made a face that suggested she was nuts. She giggled. "Are you afraid?"

Eric scoffed at the suggestion that he would be afraid of anything. He shrugged and removed his shirt. His friends asked what the hell he was doing and he told them to relax. He hesitated for a moment, trying to steady his heart, which was hammering in his chest. He was a good swimmer, but this was the sea after all. The life ring was there though, and if this girl could manage the tide then he was sure he could too. He dived in.

He broke the surface, grinning, pleased with himself. He was sure that diving in was some sort of test to this woman, and he had passed. He searched her face, wondering why he didn't recognise her. He'd spent a lot of time at the beach, most of it checking out the women who often went there. But this girl was a stranger.

"Are you from Cornwall?" he asked. "I thought I knew everyone round here but I would never forget a face like yours."

She smiled and swam around him in a circle, and with speed that both impressed him and made him nervous.

"You remind me of someone," she replied.

"A model?" he teased. "I get that a lot. I'm Eric."

At that, she threw her head back and laughed. He felt nervous again, but not so nervous that he was about to get out of the water and pass up this opportunity. He smiled at her, wondering what was so funny. This girl was weird, but damn, she was beautiful. He was trying to look without it being obvious, but he was pretty sure she was swimming naked too.

"No wonder I was drawn to you. I knew an Eric once, long ago," she told him.

"Oh yeah? Was he as good-looking as me?" Eric winked at her, feeling pretty confident that he was in with a shot. It was rare that he missed when it came to things like this.

"You look just like him, you're surely a descendent?" she replied. Something sad flickered in her eyes, but only for a moment.

"Bet he didn't have his own yacht though, did he?" Eric asked. She looked at his boat, unimpressed.

"He was a prince."

That shut Eric up for a minute because he didn't know how to respond to that. He couldn't tell if she was messing with him, or trying to make him feel inferior to her former boyfriend, but either way, he didn't like it.

"How about we get back on board?"

"He was my whole world until he saw all of me," she continued, ignoring him. She sounded sad now, and Eric was getting bored. He looked back up at his friends, who were staring at him in disbelief. He didn't notice that as well as sad, she was now angry. Eric wrapped one arm around the life ring and grabbed her around the waist with the other. Her eyes suddenly went dark.

"Unhand me."

He laughed at her phrasing and shook his head, pulling her closer. He smirked; she was definitely naked.

"Come on babe, have a drink with me and I'll take you out when we get back to shore."

She struggled against him and he was surprised at how strong she was.

"I don't belong there!" she protested, angry.

"Everyone belongs on dry land, sweetheart," Eric laughed. "Pull us up, boys!"

"That's just what he said," she seethed, "before he tried to hunt me down." She tried to wriggle out of his grasp as his friends drew them in. Eric rolled his eyes, fed up of hearing her melodramatic account of this other guy.

"Where's your boyfriend now then, babe?"

She laughed again, a cold and cruel sound that made him shiver. She gestured out to the sea.

"Oh, he's here."

Eric considered loosening his grip on her but didn't. He normally had a short attention span when it came to women, and his interest in her was alternating between irritation and intrigue. She was hot but she was clearly not right in the head, and what did she mean 'he's here'? He would never admit it to anyone, but she was creeping him out. However, he wasn't about to let her go. She'd drown out here on her own, and he'd be held responsible for just sailing off and leaving her. If he took her back though, he'd probably be hailed a hero. He liked the sound of that. He tightened his grip on her.

"Let me go!" she screamed, thrashing at him. Something seemed to kick out at him, but it didn't feel like feet. It was something slimy. He looked at her infuriated face and her eyes were now almost completely black. "You really are just the same."

"Pull us up, now!" he yelled to his friends, not even trying to mask the fear in his voice. What was wrong with her? She made one last attempt to wriggle free, failed, and then smiled at him. He recognised the threat and this time he let go, but it was too late because now she was holding on to him.

Eric treaded water in the pitch black again as the images disappeared, but he could still hear her voice singing her song, then her laughter. It wasn't a dream at all, but a memory.

"Who are you? What do—"

"Who are you? What do you want? *What* are you?" she interrupted, mocking him. "You ask the same questions every time."

He shivered, but not just with the cold. Those other memories were probing at him now, trying to show themselves. He didn't want to see them. He didn't want to know the rest of what he'd forgotten. He knew now that those blurry memories would show him a worse truth than what he believed he was already living.

"My friends will..."

"'My friends will come back for me'," she laughed, imitating his voice. "Your friends stopped looking for you years ago."

His lungs filling with water, the unbearable pressure in his chest.

He knew now why the absolute darkness felt so familiar, even though it shouldn't. Why he felt so used to the cold.

"No," he half-croaked, half-whimpered.

"Yes," she hissed. "Please let me go," she cried,

mimicking him again. She laughed and it was sharp and cruel.

"You belong to the sea now," they both said. He remembered now, he remembered all of it. Every time he'd drowned and every time he'd awoken under water, confused and terrified, frantically kicking back up to the surface. Every time was as painful, as terrifying, as the first.

She would never let him go. She would never let him die.

His body, racked with exhaustion and aching and cramping, gave up. Too weak to stop it, he slipped beneath the waves, crying and hoping that this time would be different, that this time he wouldn't come back.

Eric treaded water, kicking his legs in wide arcs. He didn't know how long he had been bobbing in the waves alone. He didn't remember how he had come to be in the water in the first place. All he remembered was that he had initially come out on a boat. But it was gone now. All that there was, all that he could see for miles and miles in every direction, was sea.

It Never Feels Like Drowning

Damien Angelica Walters

The coastline here, all craggy, plunging cliffs and white-whipped froth, would never fly back home. They'd ugly it up with metal barricades and huge warning signs that inevitably wouldn't deter the driven or the thrill seekers or eager candidates for the Darwin Awards. They'd build a theme park nearby with expensive day-passes, kiddie rides and roller coasters, and a massive parking lot. Souvenirs and sunburns. Or, Bree thought, tipping her chin toward the clouded sky, maybe not so much the latter.

Easier for her to think about things like that. About rubbish and nonsense. Easier than thinking about the arrangements she was here to finalize. Easier than thinking about her sister.

She stared out – not down – at the grey-green water, the waves crashing on the rocks a cudgel to her heart. Once again, she was sweeping in to tidy a mess Mikayla left behind. But this time, Bree didn't have to be afraid. Nothing could hurt her. A pinch of relief nestled in her breastbone and felt the worst sort of betrayal. It wasn't even a fair thought; it had been years since she'd been at risk. She touched the small scar above her right eyebrow. No one's fault. She'd been young and had gotten too close, hadn't fully grasped the inherent danger.

"Bree, come away from there, please?"

Mark, her boyfriend of three years, stood twenty feet away, his face as white as the foam below. She wanted to tell him she was fine, she wasn't that close to the edge, but she wasn't and she was, so she stepped back until his shoulders let go of their tension.

He took her in his arms, and while a curious numbness had fallen over her as soon as they'd landed at Heathrow, she still welcomed his touch. A hundred yards from the cliff sat Lavender House, the reason her sister had come to England in the first place. A bequest from a great-aunt neither knew in life. A six bedroom behemoth with a peaked roof, widow's walk, and a wide porch. A little run-down, but nothing a bit of money and time couldn't fix. *A bed and breakfast, Bree, can't you just see it?*

They'd flipped a coin to see who'd come to see if it was viable, never mind that they had plenty of pictures and reports from an agent. The toss was really only a formality. Bree wouldn't have been able to come for several more months because of work, and Mikayla wanted to start yesterday, the way she always did with everything.

Bree's bosses were far more understanding with respect to a death in the family.

"The realtor is coming this afternoon, right?" Mark said against the top of her head.

"Uh-huh, but they're called estate agents here."

He laughed. "Same difference. Are you hungry? Want me to make some breakfast? If I can figure out how to work the stove anyway."

She nodded. He offered to take care of the dishes

after, something she gladly accepted. She wandered through the first floor of the house, catching glimpses of her sister everywhere – four wavy streaks in the dust atop the mahogany buffet in the dining area, the half-open curtains in the parlor, books pulled halfway from the library's shelves. And in the bedroom upstairs, her clothes, her hairbrush with long blonde strands still caught in the bristles, her open suitcase. Her prescription bottles.

They'd arrived at the house late last night, leaving their luggage in the foyer and taking the only suitable space. She'd had a brief moment to breathe in her sister on pillow and duvet – funny how they always chose the same side of the bed, the one furthest from the door – and then she was out for the count.

She hadn't noticed that everything was mussed in a way that said police, not Mikayla. Bree had spoken to the Detective Inspector a few times on the phone. He'd seemed kind and patient, but there'd been no point in arguing or causing a fuss. Not even when they called off the search for a body. They'd seen the medication, had known what it was for. A few other phone calls had revealed her history, the other attempts. The investigation was finished, the inquest done. The official story: suicide. Mikayla, another statistic in a long line of the same, all driven to the edge by shadows they couldn't escape.

And lest there'd be any doubt, she'd left a note.

Perched on the edge of the bed, she opened that note now, left at the house by DI Lewis. He'd read it over the phone, but seeing her sister's words, her handwriting, sent a shudder through her.

Dear Bree:
I can't do it anymore. I'm tired of fighting them, tired of
everything. It hurts too much.
I'm sorry.
M.

Them. No one else would understand what she'd really meant. They'd make their own assumptions. And they'd be wrong.

Bree had killed Mikayla's first shadow before she started kindergarten. It was small and easily squished to ruin beneath a light-up sneaker, a thought that now struck her as almost funny. But only almost.

They'd been playing in the backyard. Mikayla suddenly bent over, whimpering and pulling at her hair, her clothes. As Bree opened her mouth to call for their mother, Mikayla started coughing deep in her chest, and a small darkness slipped from her lips, like a short ribbon of charcoal-colored bile. Without thought, Bree stomped one small foot. The thump of her sole, a small wet squish, and only a dark smudge remained, similar to the guts of an insect. And it was done. They looked at each other with wide eyes, Mikayla no longer crying. The roles were set in that instant. Whenever Mikayla felt one trying to emerge, she would find Bree and tug her hand. Bath or basement, yard or crawl space, anywhere at all. With each passing year, the shadows grew larger and larger, but Bree was always at the ready. Shoes, a rolled newspaper, a baseball bat. Whatever it took to destroy them. Until a few months after Mikayla's thirteenth birthday, when she stopped sicking them up.

"I can't," she told Bree. "I feel them in me, and I try and try but they won't come out."

Syrup of ipecac, a finger shoved down the throat, nothing they tried worked.

"It'll be okay," Bree promised. What else could she say? But even at fifteen, she sensed her words were lies. Sensed Mikayla knew it, too.

From that point on, Mikayla changed. She jumped at nothing, shrank from things unseen, withdrew tightly into herself, and stayed in her bedroom with headphones turned to the highest volume. And all the doctors and the pills in the world couldn't fix her. And neither could Bree. No matter how many nights she crept into her sister's room, trying in vain to help her vomit. To make her better.

No one knew the truth except for the girls and their mother, and she took off not long after she carried in a pile of laundry and saw what they were doing. They'd managed to keep it a secret from their father until his death the previous year.

Bree folded the note and tucked it away. Over the years, Mikayla had tried pills, a knife to her wrists, and once Bree caught her carefully reading the label on a bottle of drain cleaner. Mikayla was always as strong as she *could* be. The shadows were stronger. But a few years ago, everything had seemed to get better. Maybe it was the right combination of meds, maybe it had all finally run its course. Or maybe she'd simply gotten better at hiding the darkness from her sister.

The door chimes rang, a melody Bree felt she should recognize but didn't. The estate agent was already familiar with the place, didn't need anything other than a few signatures.

"How long will you be staying," the agent asked as she was placing the documents in her satchel.

"Not long," Bree said. "We'll be leaving as soon as I finish all...this."

Sorrow danced across the agent's face and Bree extended a hand, wanting her gone. Soon enough, she was on her way, with the reminder that it might take quite a bit of time before they – *she* – found an interested buyer, because of cliff erosion. "Sad to say, it's the whole coastline," she said.

Mark was in the library, tucked in a leather chair. He started to rise when she entered, but she stayed him with a hand.

"I'm going for a walk," she said.

"Do you..."

"No. I won't be long, just need to clear my head a bit."

She went back to the cliff's edge, back to the water, and this time, she looked down. Five hundred feet or near enough. All that force, all that relentless energy. All those jagged rocks concealed and then revealed, like a softly draping cowl across a woman's decolletage. How bad must it have been for Mikayla to jump? "Fuck you," she muttered to the water, her words swallowed by the crash and hiss.

The pale sun vanished behind a cloud, turning the grey day even darker, the water murky and mottled. Bree shivered in the chill, grimacing. And to think that this was spring.

Mark was still in the library when she returned. She pretended the walk had been more beneficial than it really had been, and he accepted her words as fact. She suspected it only a polite fiction on his part as well, but it was appreciated. The last thing she needed was to be picked apart and dissected for weak spots.

She fell asleep to the rhythmic pounding of the surf and woke in the middle of the night to the same. For a few moments, her fingers clutched at the sheets, but the disorientation ebbed. She rolled on her side, Mark's steady breathing a comfort. A gust of wind rattled the eaves. The light from the bath across the hall didn't penetrate the corners of the room, making it seem so much smaller than it really was.

A strange sound, oddly liquid and wavery, came from somewhere in the distance. She bolted upright, one hand reaching for Mark's shoulder, fingers a hair's breadth from his skin, head cocked to the side. The house creaked and groaned as it settled deeper into its bones. The waves pounded the cliff. *Pull yourself together*, she told herself as she sank into the too-soft mattress. Still, though, she rubbed away goosebumps as she listened to the house, and the sun was lightening the edges of the window when she finally fell asleep.

Mark had coffee ready when she came downstairs. On the counter near the stove, there were several canisters of tea that must've belonged to the great-aunt, because neither she nor Mikayla cared for it. She was halfway through her coffee when she shoved away from the table, crossed the room, and one by one upended the containers into the trash can, leaves spilling with a soft patter. After only a moment's consideration, the canisters went in as well.

When she returned to her chair, Mark cleared his throat. "What was that for?"

"I have to start somewhere, don't I?" With straightened arms, she rubbed her hands together under the table.

"I guess so." He gave her a half-smile. "Did you sleep okay?"

"Of course not," she said, her words sharper than she intended. "How could I?"

He poured another cup of coffee at the counter and she wrapped her arms under his, pressed her cheek between his shoulder blades. "I'm sorry."

"If it makes you feel better, I didn't sleep well either. This house...way too old and noisy."

Bree laughed softly against his back. "Very much so."

"What do you want to do today?"

She swallowed hard before answering. "I want to pack Mikayla's things."

"Do you want some help?"

She shook her head. "No, but when I'm done, could you arrange to have them shipped home?"

"Of course."

"In case I forget, thank you. For everything, but mostly for being here."

He gave her hands a squeeze. "Where else would I be?"

She finished her second cup of coffee and had a third, but when that was finished, she couldn't delay any further. The staircase seemed narrower. Back in the bedroom, the walls loomed closer, the ceiling lower, the floor ready to pull her under. She fisted her hands and took long, deep breaths.

Mikayla's medication took a trip down the toilet, requiring multiple flushes. Her clothes were folded into neat piles, her shoes tucked into plastic bags. A thriller with a dog-eared page remained on the nightstand. The sight of that folded edge, of knowing her sister would never know the answer to the mystery within, brought forth a fresh wash of tears. Subtle movement registered in the corner of Bree's eye and she wiped her sorrow away with a forearm. "Yes?"

No answer.

She turned to find the space as empty as it had been. There was something muted – a footfall? – from the hallway.

"Mark?" she said, her voice shrill.

Again, no answer.

The hall was empty. So, too, the staircase and the rooms at the front of the house. Mark was in the kitchen, sending a text message, steam from a fresh cup of coffee curling in the air.

"Everything okay?" he asked, his brow creased.

"Were you upstairs a minute ago?"

"No, why?"

"I thought I heard someone." She rubbed her upper arms. "Just more house noise, I guess."

His face softened. His tone, too. "If it's too much, I can pack everything."

"No, it's fine. Honestly, I'm almost done. She didn't bring that much." Tears burned but she blinked them away and returned to the second floor. When she finished, save for a stack of papers with sketches and snippets of what first appeared to be poetry, she gave everything over to Mark and he left to find packing materials and a post office.

The house seemed darker, more closed off when she was alone and she wandered through, pressing fingers and palms to walls and furniture. The sensation of being watched settled on her shoulders, a shawl of unease. In the library, Mark hadn't touched the books Mikayla had pulled halfway out. Now, Bree went through and tucked them in until their spines aligned with their neighbors, even though she was only going to have to pull them out again to box them up. She'd just fixed a copy of *Alice's Adventures in Wonderland* when from deep in the house, a noise. A laugh?

She froze in place, fingers spread, lips parted. It wasn't Mark's laugh; not his genuinely happy, nor his to humor you, nor his intoxicated revelry laugh. Maybe it wasn't a laugh at all. The spell in her limbs broke and she moved, whisper-soft and feather fall-slow, to the door, keeping just inside but craning her neck to listen.

"Mark?" she called, wincing at how loud her voice seemed, and yet how small when compared to the house. She gnawed a cuticle. "Mikayla?" Her voice broke in the middle. She pinched the bridge of her nose. Knuckled her upper lip.

With a grunt, she returned to the shelves. A bookseller the agent had recommend was coming tomorrow to look for first or early editions, the rest to be donated to a local library – another agent suggestion. The day after, a dealer in antiquities was coming to look at the furniture. Once those things were taken care of, a service was coming in to survey the house to give an estimate for a deep cleaning, and she had a meeting with a local couple who'd be caretaking the house until it sold.

And then? Home, to take care of Mikayla's apartment.

She left the library and visited the unoccupied bedrooms. Bedframes without mattresses, dressers adorned with dusty picture frames containing black and white histories of someone else's life, wardrobes with neatly folded blankets and, in the smallest at the very end of the hall, a satin gown the color of the Caribbean. A mirror stood in the corner and she held the dress in front of her, swaying from side to side, the hem sliding along the floor with a gentle susurration.

She stopped moving. The dress stilled. The whisper continued.

Whirling around, she left the gown in a puddle on the wood. Mark's name lodged in her throat, a dry-swallowed pill. One step, then another, on wooden feet of apprehension and fear. And the sound... Fabric on wood or water running over a stone. Soft, but pervasive. Moving further away, albeit slowly.

The front door opened with a bang. "I'm back!"

She yelped and ran down the steps, skin slipping on the treads, hand holding tight to the railing to keep from tumbling to the bottom. She ran into his arms without stopping and burst into tears.

"What's wrong?"

"I just, I heard—" More tears and then laughter as embarrassment washed over her. "My mind was playing tricks on me and—" More laughter, and was there an edge of the hysterical? She thought there might be.

He pulled her close, kissed her forehead and held her tight, and when his arms finally loosened, she felt better. Mostly.

They finished the day by boxing all the knick-knacks and photographs and wiping dust from the flat surfaces. Evening baths for both left a grey halo of grime on the porcelain tub. A storm rolled in just before they turned in, filling the house with the rage of the wind and ocean. Mark fell asleep quickly, but Bree tossed and turned. A gust of wind shook the window shutters and she flopped on her side, facing the interior wall.

The light in the bath flickered once, twice, and went out. Bree held her breath and closed her eyes. Silly, perhaps. Darkness reigned there, too. Slowly, she slitted her lids open. Lightning strobed the room, bright enough to reveal someone in the doorway.

She sat up with a yelp, spine jamming hard against the bedframe, shaking Mark awake at the same time.

"Huh?" he said, voice thick with sleep.

"Someone's here," she hissed, her fingers talons.

The lightning flashed again. The entry was empty.

"They were standing right there. Watching us."

Mark thumped out of bed and she tried to pull him back, but her fingers touched air instead. She pawed for the light pull on the bedside lamp; the yellow glow went on at the same time Mark stepped out. She slid from the bed to follow.

He turned on the overhead in the hallway and they went room to room, closing each door once they'd finished checking. The tension in Bree's shoulders lessened a bit with each one, but when they took to the stairs to the first floor, her muscles tightened again. They took a slow circuit, turning on lights until the place was daylight bright, double-checking all the locks. They ended in the kitchen, which was as empty as everywhere else. Outside, the lightning and thunder spaced further and further apart and the wind ceased its howling.

"I swear I thought I saw someone," Bree said, her voice small.

"It's okay," he said. "Are *you* okay?"

She shook her head, her words too tangled to emerge.

They stood in the kitchen, arms wrapped round each other, until finally he said, "Let's go back to bed."

"I doubt I'll be able to sleep," she said.

But, eventually, she did.

They slept in, and Bree had just finished dressing when the bookseller, a thin woman with long, white hair and Doc Martens, arrived. The woman worked quickly, creating multiple piles in the library, and when she finished, she took several boxes with her and left a check. Bree and Mark loaded the rest of the books into the rental car and followed the agent's directions to the library. Afterward, they had dinner in town at a small restaurant with dark paneled walls and dim lighting and by the time they got back to the house, they were yawning fiercely.

Still, though, before they turned in, Mark walked through the house and made certain everything was secure. Bree knew it was for her benefit and loved him even more for it. They fell asleep curled together in the bed, like two snails sharing the same shell, the light from the bath peeking in.

But Bree woke in darkness. No storm, no wind. She reached for Mark but withdrew her hand and exhaled through her nose. The light bulb probably burned out. No reason to wake him. No reason to be alarmed. She snuggled closer, his body warm against hers. In the distance, the soft conversation of the ocean. Drawing closer, growing louder.

And louder still.

Too loud.

Sitting, she fumbled on the bedside lamp. The ceiling was too close, too low. She slid down until she was flat. It wasn't the ceiling. Above, darkness stretched from end to end, a foot lower than the plaster it concealed. It moved and shifted, pulsing slowly, the rhythmic, liquid noise accompanying each movement.

She elbowed Mark. "Wake up," she said, barely moving her lips.

"What?"

"Shhh. Look up. No, don't sit, just look."

"What the—"

But she knew, oh yes, she knew. Mikayla might have gone over the cliff, but she'd left something behind. Not intentionally, no. Her sister would never do that to her. The shadows, rats deserting a sinking ship. Too large for a shoe or even a baseball bat. Had they been waiting for this moment for years? Planning for it?

Mark slowly scooted to the edge of the bed, pulling her with him. Together, they slipped onto the floor, attention focused overhead. The pulse, the hum, continued. They scuttled toward the door and the darkness descended another foot. Bree moaned against flatlined lips.

Inch by inch, they closed the distance between bed and exit and Mark had one hand on the jamb when the shadows dropped yet again. He shoved her out and quickly followed.

"Go, go," he shouted, yanking her up.

In the hallway, their feet tattooed the wood with fear and fury. Around them, more shadows began to peel off the walls. Strangely shaped with many limbs, creeping inexorably toward them on floor and baseboard with that terrible wet, slippery murmur.

"Hurry, hurry, hurry," Bree urged.

Their passage on the staircase was marked with a series of erratic thumps. When they reached the bottom, they raced toward the door. Through the foyer and then out; a pinch of sunrise on the horizon pinking the sky. As the door slammed shut, the inhuman hum silenced and relief pricked the edges of her mind. Then it returned.

She didn't want to look, to know, but she couldn't *not*. Shadows were melting from the windows, charcoal veils spilling down the sides and pooling on the ground.

Bree and Mark ran toward the car. Movement to her right. A long shadow speared through the grass with the sound of wheat caught in a strong wind, and she pushed Mark to the left to avoid it. The shadow split in two, piercing the green between their feet. Cutting them off from each other. Cutting *her* off from the car.

She shrieked and stumbled to her knees, her fingertips scant inches from the murk. Mark reached for her, but the shadow widened, forcing him away from her. Forcing her back, too.

And back and back.

Pebbles dug into her arches, the tips of her toes. Mark's arm was still extended, mouth contorted in horror, panicked rendering his gaze wild as he scanned in all directions for a way to reach her that no longer existed. The darkness pushed. She moved. Heading toward the cliff's edge, being *herded* toward the edge.

"What do you want from me!" she shrieked through her tears.

She'd always thought they lacked intelligence, acting on something akin to instinct. But this didn't feel like instinct. This felt intentional. This felt personal. The realization was acid on her tongue.

"You can't do this," she sobbed. "I'm sorry! I'm sorry!"

She took mincing, baby steps. The darkness surged, forcing her to hasten her pace. Mark was too far to help, but she screamed for him nonetheless, screamed until her throat burned and her voice rasped.

The shadows continued their slow and steady advance. Behind and below, the sea crashed against the rocks again and again and again.

And Fade Out Again

Thana Niveau

The only thing stronger than mankind's compulsion to destroy itself was the determination that it would endure. Like a virus, it adapted. It survived.

Stefani watched the colours, luminescent in the glow from the sun lamps. The light was artificial, but the surrounding coral didn't seem to mind. It was the only thing truly thriving in the poisoned ocean. If you didn't count the city.

By the time the human race had finally decided to stop killing each other, the planet was nearly uninhabitable. It was too late to reverse the effects of global warming. The polar ice caps were long gone and the seas had risen, drowning cities, countries and finally entire continents. Most of the land was gone, as were any hopes of escaping to the stars to find and colonise other worlds. The space program had drowned along with most of the planet.

Stefani couldn't imagine what it must have been like living above the surface. VR tech could approximate the experience of wandering through forests or deserts, but it all seemed so unnatural, and the animals that had once lived up there were terrifying and strange. She had never known life outside the maternal embrace of the superocean and the comforting womb of New Eden.

Once the world above had reached the point of no return, scientists and architects had focused their efforts on the world below. Or rather, the world that would soon *be* below. And the Eden Project in Cornwall was a perfect starting point.

The huge geodesic domes housed both a tropical rainforest and a Mediterranean environment. Over a period of months, the structures were essentially uprooted and a giant foundation constructed beneath them. At the same time, teams of underwater engineers and computer programmers combined their efforts in revolutionary 3D printing technology, constructing a giant bubble of metallic glass to form an underwater habitat. Detractors called it the Goldfish Bowl, and for a while the name stuck. But New Eden was the official name.

As the seas continued to rise, the British coast was devastated by flooding and erosion. The Doomsday Clock ticked away the dwindling time as the waves lapped closer and closer, engulfing the Cornish countryside. In a few short months, the bubble was completely submerged and a maze of corridors and rooms branched off in every direction. A titanium auger spiralled down through the centre of the habitat, anchoring it to the seabed, and the weight of the water provided all the energy the city needed. And at the top, the domes floated like manmade islands, their hexagonal panels reinforced to filter the deadly rays of the sun through the depleted atmosphere. The plants and trees within would have to sustain what remained of the human race.

The other major food was fish. Specifically, lionfish.

The notoriously invasive species was once considered a major threat to marine ecosystems, and the lionfish's unchecked proliferation had altered the balance of life beneath the waves long before the catastrophic flooding that drowned the world. Thousands of other species had died out, and scientists could only speculate how widespread the lionfish were throughout the rest of the superocean. But until they overpopulated themselves out of existence, they provided an unlimited food source.

Once Britain had been fully subsumed by the ocean, the reef began to establish itself. First the coral covered the remaining features of the Eden Project – the visitor centre, restaurant and sculptures. Then it spread outward into the towns and villages, and finally the habitat, blanketing everything as it had once engulfed shipwrecks and other structures. It was a living organism as vibrant as the terrestrial forests and jungles once had been. It made a home of anything it found in the sea. Like humans, it colonised. And like humans, it learned and adapted.

The doomsayers fretted about structural collapse. The reef was consuming New Eden, they said. In time it would crush the entire habitat, level by level. And yes, the older parts of the structure were beginning to show signs of stress. But the printers worked day and night to keep extending the city. If and when the reef did overrun them, they had the rest of the ocean to spread out in. There were even plans to start a new city, one entirely independent of New Eden.

Stefani listened to the buzz of the printers as she ran through the routine systems check of the machines. The newest corridor was growing fast. A special airlock would keep it isolated from the water until it was completed. Then the structural engineers would move in, performing rigorous stress tests until the area was declared safe and could be opened to the population.

This particular corridor would lead to a new housing wing, where Stefani had reserved a place. Her apartment was in the oldest part of the city, and it was beginning to show its age. The surrounding glass was cloudy and scratched, due to be recycled as soon as the new wing was completed. As much as she loved her view of the giant bee sculpture blanketed in coral, her view of the reef would be much better from one of the modern developments.

Many people found it oppressive on the seabed, but Stefani had never been claustrophobic. On the contrary, she felt safe, cocooned in the smaller rooms of the original construction. In this tiny corner of what was once the British Isles, mankind had made history. First with the Eden Project itself, and then with the city.

The vibrations of the machinery often attracted animals and today was no exception. The eel was back. Stefani watched as the gleaming yellow creature slithered past, its mouth opening to show rows of teeth. It paused to snap up a bright orange clownfish that had left the sanctuary of the coral. Stefani pressed a hand against the glass as she watched the eel. Supposedly there had once been similar animals on land, immense snakes that could swallow a person whole. She'd seen images of them, but to her they were like dinosaurs must have seemed to her forefathers. Beautiful, deadly animals one could scarcely even imagine.

A pride of lionfish was prowling nearby and for a moment the eel looked poised to attack. But the lionfish flared their venomous spines, making themselves appear larger than they were. The display was enough to change the eel's mind. With a flick of its golden tail, it was gone, away into the depths.

"Goodbye, Sunray," Stefani said. "Bring your family next time."

From behind her came a soft laugh. She turned to see Aren standing there, shaking his head.

"What?"

"Did you name all the lionfish too, Stef?"

She grinned at his teasing tone. "Not all of them. But then, they're not as friendly. Plus I don't like to eat the ones I chat to."

Aren looked out into the water and Stef followed his gaze into the vibrantly colourful reef. For a while they watched in silence as different fish darted in amongst the anemones and coral. Tiny moon jellyfish pulsed in the gentle current, transforming the void into a starry underwater sky.

"I never get tired of watching," Stef said.

Aren sighed. "I was sick of it after the first five minutes down here."

Stef stared at him in disbelief. "Really?"

"Really. Nothing ever changes. Same reef, same fish. Same bloody *lionfish*. I saw a shark once, but it didn't look anything like I expected. I thought they were supposed to be these huge monsters, vicious killers. It was smaller than me and it just swam by, as bored as I was."

For long moments Stef was at a loss for words. There

was nothing at all boring about the reef or its inhabitants. But then, Aren normally worked in the rainforest. He'd told her before that fish weren't as interesting to a botanist as plants were. You couldn't interact with the reef the way you could with things in the dome.

She watched as he cupped his hands around his face, peering through the glass at the undersea world.

"Without diving gear," he said, "that's as close as you can get to the reef. In the dome you can climb trees, pick flowers, even let bees and butterflies clamber over you. You can talk to plants and see them respond. Down here you're just a watcher. Passive." He shook his head sadly.

Ah. Now she understood. What were they thinking, exiling someone like Aren to the lower decks?

"Do you name all the trees and bees and flowers up top?" she asked.

Aren turned away from the glass, the hint of a smile threatening to overtake his gloomy expression. "Nothing *ever* gets you down, does it?"

Stef blushed and looked back out into the water. "I don't know," she mumbled. "Maybe. Sometimes."

There was a ping as one of the printers finished a circuit of the corridor and reversed direction to begin another. Stef glanced at the readings on the wall screen.

"All good," she said cheerfully.

"Yeah, that's the problem down here," Aren said. "It's *always* good. Always the same. Like the reef. Nothing ever changes. Print, print, print. Another corridor. Start again. Another hatch. Another wing. And the *noise*." He pressed his hands against his temples. "I just wish I could leave."

"Leave? You mean move to a new apartment? A new wing?"

"No. A new city. Above the water."

Stef frowned. The very thought was so alien, so *terrifying*.

"I just feel it pressing in," Aren continued. "The reef." His voice was low and conspiratorial, as though he was afraid of being overheard. "Every day it obscures more and more of the glass. It's like it wants to get inside. Crush this insignificant little bubble and rid the planet of the last of our industry. We weren't meant to be down here."

Stef shifted uncomfortably. It wasn't like Aren to be so morose. She'd been delighted when they'd first assigned him to work with her. Aren was like her – friendly and outgoing. But after only a handful of days on the seabed, his mood had changed. Now his words had an eerily familiar ring to them.

Her workstation sat against one curved wall of the little room. It was surrounded by coral, encrusted by the stony exoskeletons of millions of sea creatures. The divers had cleared away a large circular portion so she could see out into the water, and the area where she sat for most of the day gave the illusion of being part of the reef itself. It was beautiful, comforting – not at all like the domes. Up there it was too bright. There was too much space, too much openness. You were too close to the sun up there, too close to its poisonous rays and heat.

"Look," she said, "I know there's always supposed to be two people here, but this isn't the right posting for you, even if it is only temporary. I can call for help if

180 | *Thana Niveau*

anything goes wrong. It's not fair to make you cover for someone in another station."

Aren dragged his fingers through his hair, shaking his head. "No, no," he said. "You know the rules. I can't leave you here by yourself."

"Yeah, I know the rules. And I'm telling you it's okay to break them. The printers have only slowed a little bit; they haven't stopped. And they won't. These new precautions are nothing but administrative overprotectiveness. I'm fine here on my own. I *like* it here."

Of course she knew the real reason he was reluctant to go. It was the same reason she found his sudden pessimism so disturbing. She met his eyes and added firmly, "I'm not like Dunkan. What happened to him would never happen to me."

Aren glanced out into the water again. Lionfish were swarming over a cluster of Gorgonian sea fans, darting in and out as they plucked tiny creatures from the delicate structures.

"Pygmy seahorses," she said, allowing a trace of wistfulness into her voice.

Aren winced and turned away.

Another printer signalled its completion, and the vibrations took on a higher tone as it began the more detailed work of constructing the door hatch.

Stef placed her hands on Aren's shoulders. "Go," she said. "I don't need help to keep an eye on the printers. And I don't need companionship. Solitude and monotony don't bother me. In fact, it's how I like it. Go tell your supervisor a robot could do my job."

He met that with a wry laugh. "Careful or you'll make yourself obsolete." His eyes flicked across to the sunroom, the little chamber he'd retreated to every hour for a dose of artificial sun. The real sunlight never reached this far down.

Stef registered the look, and he noticed her noticing.

"All right," he said at last. "If you're sure..."

"I'm sure."

He cast one final look out at the reef, then turned to go. He hesitated at the door, then murmured "Thank you" before slipping away down the corridor and out of sight.

Stef was alone again. She sighed as she sat down. Already the room felt larger, emptier. She would miss Aren's company, but she couldn't stand to see him suffer. And he *was* suffering. Very few people were suited to life at the bottom of New Eden. She took trips up to the biomes from time to time. But she preferred the synthetic floor to the dirt, and the water to the sky. The habitat was all she'd ever known, and all she needed.

Unlike Stef, most people needed the bright world above. Some went mad without it. A flicker of disquiet ran through her and she tried to push the memory Aren had evoked to the back of her mind. But it came, unbidden.

She was running late. Her shower had stopped halfway through washing her hair and she'd had to scrub away the remaining soap with a towel. She tried to call the print lab, but there was no answer. When she finally arrived, ready with a breezy apology, there was no sign of Dunkan. She found him quickly enough, though, crouched in a corner, staring around wildly. He was murmuring to himself.

"Please," he whispered, "leave me alone. Stop following me. I'm sorry."

"Dunkan? What's wrong?"

He seemed not to hear her, and kept up his frantic pleading for a few moments more.

Growing concerned, Stef knelt beside him. "Who are you talking to?"

He stared at her, his eyes wide, distraught. At last, he said in a whisper, "Mila."

Stef felt a chill at that and she glanced behind her in spite of herself. "Dunkan," she said, her voice low and calm, "Mila's not here anymore."

But his expression of fear didn't change. "Don't you think I know that?"

Stef didn't want to ask, but she had to. "Where did you see her?"

Dunkan pointed a trembling finger towards the glass, towards the cleared window of coral. "Out there."

A wave of sadness and pity washed over Stef. There was nothing out there, nothing but the reef. Mila had drowned a week ago whilst clearing away more coral from the habitat.

"I sometimes think I see things in the water too. But it's just a trick of the light, fish swimming around, turtles." But she could see her reassurances were having no effect.

"No! It was *her*, Stef. It was Mila. But her body was... it was all *wrong*. Her *eyes*..." He lowered his voice. "I think she blames me."

Stef shook her head. "What are you talking about? Blames you for what?"

He covered his face with his hands. "I saw it. Saw *her*, I mean, when she..." He began to cry then, murmuring Mila's name over and over.

Stef didn't know what to say. She stood up, looking out into the water as she tried to imagine what Dunkan had seen. She supposed it was possible that Mila's body – or some of it – was still floating out there, but it wouldn't comfort Dunkan to be told that the sea and its inhabitants had most likely consumed her by now. He knew that anyway. Like everything else in New Eden, the dead were recycled, returned to the sea.

"I know what you're thinking, Stef."

"What?"

"That there's nothing left of her."

Stef turned back to him, unnerved that he seemed to have read her mind. But then, what else could she have been thinking? After a few moments of silence, she said, "It's true. There *can't* be anything left. You know that."

Dunkan nodded slowly, his expression darkening. "I know. The fish eat us and we eat the fish. We've become cannibals."

It was a sickening leap in logic. Even so, she felt her stomach lurch at the thought. "Dunkan..."

"And why not? We devoured everything else on the planet. We started as we meant to go on. We're like that ugly reef out there, taking over everything, grinding it down, destroying it."

"But we work *with* the reef," Stef protested. She was

desperate to derail his morbid train of thought. "It's what keeps us alive. It *saved* us."

"No. It's killing us. Like it killed Mila." He paused, taking a long shuddering breath. "I saw her die."

Stef blinked. He hadn't said anything about that at the time. Only Ling, Mila's diving partner, had witnessed her fate. One of her hoses had snagged on the reef, trapping her behind Ling, who had only turned back at the last minute to see Mila struggling with her regulator. And by then it was too late. Her air was gone, leaked into the surrounding sea.

"Why didn't you tell anyone?" Stef asked softly.

Dunkan looked at her, misery etched on his face. "It didn't matter, did it? There was nothing I could have done. I stood right here and watched her drown."

Stef remembered the day well. If it had happened ten minutes earlier, she might have been the one to witness Mila's final moments instead. But she'd been topping up the thermoplastics in the printers, two rooms away.

Dunkan turned his head slowly, peering out into the reef again. "But now she's back."

The room felt chilly, and Stef wrapped her arms around herself as she stared into the murky water beyond the glass.

"If she truly is back," she ventured, choosing her words carefully, "then maybe she's telling you not to feel guilty."

The silence her words fell into was icy cold. And colder still was the look in Dunkan's eyes. He slowly got to his feet, glaring as he loomed over her. "Don't patronise me. I know what I saw."

For a moment it looked as if fury would triumph over fear, and Stef found herself edging away. But then his expression softened and he turned away, covering his face once more.

"She's out there," he whimpered. "She's coming back. They all are."

Dunkan had been taken to the infirmary, and that was the last anyone saw of him. By the time Stef went to visit him, he was gone. A notebook was later found in his quarters, filled with wild scribbling and repeated apologies, mostly to Mila. In between were frankly apocalyptic rantings, along with what the doctors called survivor's guilt. It wasn't difficult to guess what had happened.

A new rule was made that no one was to be left alone in the print lab. Stef had finally managed to push the incident to the back of her mind, but now Aren had brought it all racing back.

She closed her eyes, banishing the bad memories. She'd meant everything she said to Aren, that the solitude didn't bother her, that she was nothing like Dunkan. She wasn't prone to morbid preoccupations and she'd never seen anything in the water that shouldn't be there. Certainly not a ghost.

It was true that living below the surface wasn't natural for humans. But surely that was why they'd evolved intelligence over other species, to adapt to new and different surroundings. Before the destruction of the planet, hadn't they lived in shelters in even more challenging environments? Deserts, mountains – they'd even built a space station once.

Down here they enjoyed a symbiotic relationship with the reef. They had even begun to harvest the coral, adapting the printers to incorporate the new material. Perhaps one day new rooms would be made entirely of coral. The reef reinforced the structure of the habitat as well as providing them with food. Where Dunkan had felt trapped by it, Stef felt nurtured. The humans were doing the same thing as the reef – expanding and colonising.

The grinding of the printers was a pleasant background hum. To Stef it was the sound of life. But a sudden stutter in the mechanical droning shook her from her thoughts. She opened her eyes. And froze. Directly beyond her window was a curving arm of the reef, the same one she watched every day. It swept past the bee sculpture, up to the ruins of what had once been a concert stage. But now the coral was pushed tight against the glass. And for a moment she thought she saw a face within the waving fingers of anemone.

But it was only for a moment. Then the coral drifted away, moving on like a curious fish. Something must have broken off the piece she'd just been looking at. It happened sometimes. Storms on the surface affected the currents, even as far down as this.

She shook her head in annoyance. Aren's brooding had darkened her mood, that was all. He'd made her think of Dunkan. She turned back to the main console, pushing away her irritation before resentment could set in. It wasn't Aren's fault. But she made herself promise to be extra vigilant now that she was on her own here.

When Cassa and Min came to relieve her at the end of

her shift, she decided not to tell them anything about what she'd seen. She'd only *thought* she'd seen it, after all, and it wouldn't benefit anyone to have some momentary trick of her eyes on record.

The next few days passed without incident, and Stef was beginning to settle into her new solitary routine, enjoying the peace and quiet of having the lab to herself. Just the way she liked it. The eel greeted her occasionally, as did prides of lionfish and other creatures.

She stood before the window, gazing out into the blue. A flash of movement caught her eye and she saw to her delight that it was an octopus. The shy animal wrapped its gracefully coiling arms around the reef as it pulled itself along, pausing to camouflage itself when a large fish came too close. Stef watched until it was out of sight and then went to check the progress of the new corridor.

The printers were fine, buzzing away as usual. The readings showed a slight fluctuation and, when she investigated further, she realised that one of the storage tanks was damaged, leaking a small amount of fluid into the ocean. It could only have just happened, so she didn't feel too guilty. She entered the repair order into the system and made her way back to the main lab.

She felt it instantly. Something had changed. The room was shockingly cold and she spied a small puddle of water beside her desk. That wasn't unusual. The habitat did leak from time to time. But that wasn't what made her skin prickle.

Reluctantly, she turned towards the coral window,

and her eyes widened. Dunkan was out there, his face pressed against the glass, peering in.

For long moments she stood frozen, staring and not believing what she saw.

"You're dead," she whispered at last. "Aren't you?"

Dunkan stared back, and his lips curled in mimicry of a smile. It was an awful sight, that smile. False and unnatural.

Then she noticed his arms. His hands were cupped around his face, as though he were simply standing outside and looking in. But a third arm dangled by his side, boneless and slightly too long.

Her body was... it was all wrong. *Her* eyes...

Stef screamed.

If Dunkan heard her, he didn't react. He merely drifted there, buffeted slightly by the current, the horrible smile unwavering as he continued to stare through the glass at her.

It was as though she'd ordered the printer to craft a replica of Dunkan and it had done the best it could with only the most limited information. And Stef's heart wrenched as she began to understand at last.

Dunkan *had* seen Mila. A *replica* of her. As the printers had learned from the coral, so too had the coral learned from the printers. Whatever the invading humans left in the sea, it was beginning to reproduce.

The reef was printing too.

She ran to the back room and wrenched open the airlock door. From there she had a better view of the leaking tank. It was encrusted with spiny corals and surrounded by lionfish. They appeared to be working together to widen a puncture in the tank. Liquid polymer and plastic streamed into the water from the breach, along with the coral that had been had harvested to supplement it.

We weren't meant to be down here.

Stef sank to her knees, unable to stand upright any more. Not even the most fatalistic of scientists could have predicted this. She thought of what Aren had said about them becoming cannibals. But that wasn't entirely right. What they'd become was prey. No, it was even worse than that. They were a minor hurdle. Nothing more. The human race was simply in the way, as it always had been.

A thump sounded behind her and she slowly looked around. She wasn't surprised to see that Dunkan had followed her. He drifted just outside the airlock, his smile still frozen in place. And as she watched, he pointed towards the damaged tank with his new arm. It almost looked like he was laughing.

Stephen Bacon
stephenbacon.co.uk

Simon Bestwick
simon-bestwick.blogspot.co.uk

Georgina Bruce
georginabruce.com

Johnny Mains
johnnymains.com

Paul Meloy
facebook.com/paul.meloy

Thana Niveau
thananiveau.com

Rosalie Parker
rosalieparker.co.uk

Kit Power
patreon.com/kitpower

Guy N. Smith
guynsmith.com

Damien Angelica Walters
damienangelicawalters.com

blackshuckbooks.co.uk

Also Available

GREAT BRITISH HORROR 1

Green
and
Pleasant
Land

edited by
Steve J Shaw

Jasper Bark - A.K. Benedict - Ray Cluley
James Everington - Rich Hawkins - V.H. Leslie
Laura Mauro - Adam Millard - David Moody
Simon Kurt Unsworth - Barbie Wilde

Also Available

GREAT BRITISH HORROR 2

Dark
Satanic
Mills edited by
Steve J Shaw

Charlotte Bond - Paul Finch
Andrew Freudenberg - Gary Fry
Cate Gardner - Carole Johnstone
Penny Jones - Gary McMahon - Marie O'Regan
John Llewellyn Probert - Angela Slatter